Mary Leland is the author of the wid_____
available in Black Swan). She was bo__ ____ _____ up in Cork city
where she began her working life as a journalist for the *Cork
Examiner*. After spending some years in Dublin she returned to
Cork as a freelance writer, notably for the *Irish Times*.

She began writing fiction about ten years ago, and in 1979 some of
her first stories were published in *New Irish Writing* in the *Irish
Press*. Her work has also appeared in *Firebird 4*. *The Killeen* was
her first novel.

Mary Leland lives in Cork with her
three children.

Also by Mary Leland

THE KILLEEN

and published by Black Swan

THE LITTLE GALLOWAY GIRLS

Mary Leland

BLACK SWAN

THE LITTLE GALLOWAY GIRLS
A BLACK SWAN BOOK   0 552   99303 4

Originally published in Great Britain by Hamish Hamilton Ltd.

PRINTING HISTORY

Hamish Hamilton edition published 1987
Black Swan edition published 1988

This book is set in 11/12pt Century

Black Swan Books are published by Transworld Publishers Ltd., 61-63
Uxbridge Road, Ealing, London W5 5SA, in Australia by Transworld
Publishers (Australia) Pty. Ltd., 15-23 Helles Avenue, Moorebank, NSW
2170, and in New Zealand by Transworld Publishers (N.Z.) Ltd.,
Cnr. Moselle and Waipareira Avenues, Henderson, Auckland.

Made and printed in Great Britain by
The Guernsey Press Co. Ltd., Guernsey, Channel Islands.

For Eoin, Aoibhe, and Donal

CONTENTS

ACKNOWLEDGEMENTS

'Just Fine' first appeared in the *Irish Press;* 'Truth' appeared as 'The River Beyond Coolmore' in the *Irish Times;* 'Displaced Persons' first appeared in *The Cork Review;* 'The Swain' first appeared in the *Irish Times* Summer Series 1984; 'Internal Assonance' first appeared in the *Irish Times* Summer Series 1985; and 'Epiphany' first appeared in *Firebird 4* (Penguin).

Much of this collection was written with the assistance of a bursary from the Irish Arts Council, An Comhairle Ealaion. It is with sincere appreciation that I thank David Marcus; and also salute two of the most influential writers in Ireland, about Ireland: Ethne and Michael Viney. Warm thanks are also due to Marie and Eliz, Mary and Roxy, who helped.

The Little Galloway Girls

'Picture!' Sr Perpetua used to say. Elizabeth unconsciously echoed her as she opened the newspaper and startled her sisters with her exclamation.

'Picture!'

They gathered at the round table at which the pages were spread, and three pairs of eyes stared at the photograph and its caption: 'Lady Elizabeth Holderness presents the Gascoyne Trophy for the best Jersey bull at the Spring Show in Dublin yesterday. Accepting the prize is breeder Jeremiah Long, Longfield, Co. Down, with his bull Sherman.'

'There's no Ross!' wailed Frances, and the others smiled at her mock indignation. She was the one who was proudest of her second name – 'I'm Frances Ross Galloway, if you please,' her five-year-old self had announced on her arrival at the convent, an announcement that had gone into the annals of the school's reprobates. Up to then only the Reverend Superior had known that the two other girls were Elizabeth Holderness Galloway and Louise Gascoyne Galloway, but Frances, never again in her life to be called Fanny, had alerted the staff to the Ascendancy ring of their names.

'But the nuns all have double-barrelled names,' protested Louise when she realized how the knowledge was to be used against them. 'There's Sr Margaret of the Sacred Heart, and Mother Mary Theresa, and Sr Martin de Porres – why are they getting at us?'

Elizabeth, the eldest at eight, had been unable to explain it. It was one more manifestation of the effects

11

of the earthquake in their lives. All she had been able to do in their suddenly extraordinary circumstances was retreat totally from confrontation so as to remain the single sister not incapacitated by punishment restrictions.

This may have been partly as a result of her experience of life with their father whom, as she told them when necessary, she had known longer than they had. Her earliest emotional memory was of pity for her mother, whose bursts of resistance she witnessed, and whose despairing acquiescence she came to despise.

Contempt is a sophisticated emotion, and Elizabeth did not handle it very well. It was what distinguished her immediately among her school-fellows, and it encouraged the conclusion of the Reverend Mother that she was a devious, intractable child.

Even the Reverend Mother had to admit that there was something winning about Louise. She had a willingness to be good, to be unremarkable at least, which the nuns thought would allow her to be rescued. As for Frances – the child was young, of course, but could not be allowed to become the baby of the convent because of the strong will and obdurate, self-confident temperament immediately displayed.

Reverend Mother would be the first to admit – indeed she was – that taking three young sisters into the school all at the same time presented problems, and that the potential for trouble was emphasized by the background of the little Galloway girls. Beginning with that unfortunate, impetuous marriage – perhaps that was where Frances got her stubbornness? – and the father's life abroad while his wife reared the children in Kilkenny, well, who could wonder if, the difference in religion apart, the couple came to grief? And once that had happened, and the mother had left, how could any conscientious religious teaching community refuse the father's plea to house and educate his children?

'You can see my position, Mother Benignus,' he explained while the deal was negotiated.

'Those girls have been left to run wild. Plenty of money, I sent all I could, and there was plenty. But she never understood the rearing of children. When I was at home I tried to insist on a pattern that would remain when I had to go off again, but of course she ignored that as soon as my back was turned. And of course I asked the priest to keep an eye on the girls going to Mass and all that sort of thing, but she resented his calls and do you know, really, I think she began to resent every Catholic she knew in the end?'

Mother Benignus was shocked, of course, but she was a woman of the world if any Mother Superior was, and she knew the way things could turn out. Nor was she without heart – and besides, although she would never, ever admit it even to herself – it was all so *interesting*.

'So very young, wasn't she, Mrs Galloway? And yourself too, of course, Mr Galloway. You know, it may even turn out to be all for the best, God moves in *most* mysterious ways.'

'Oh, there were plenty to tell us we were doing the wrong thing. And I hardly knew her – hardly knew her. All we needed was to think the world against us, and we did, so there was nothing for us to do but marry and be damned to them all. With respects to you, Reverend Mother.'

'Ah, Mr Galloway. It's not the first story of that kind that I've heard. It is always hard for our young men working in England, so many of them are fooled by that gentle English charm. So sweet, of course. Anyone could understand.'

'Well.' He was curt. He knew the nun understood the economics of Catholicism, that he would be paying the bill for his daughters and that it was her business to placate him, to condole.

'Anyway. You know what I want, now. No letters from her. No visits. That's the only way. They have to be weaned. Weaned from her.'

The word with its echoes of milky maternity mocked him by its unconscious repetition.

'Separated. She isn't going to fight the case in the court so we will have a legal separation within the next six months. After that she'll have no call even to try to get here, so the important thing until then will be to keep them apart. They're still young, you know. She has influence.'

Only over her daughters, that was. And only in so far as a timid character, however kind, can have until a stronger one opposes it. Both Sr Benignus and Mr Galloway knew that pretty Mrs Galloway had no influence that mattered – no money, no family, no friends who could be called on in Ireland. The children were to be rescued from her as from the burning, saved from Anglicism as from hell.

'Picture that!' was Sr Perpetua's response to small Fanny's nomination of herself as a person of consequence, but there was no satire in the remark, no desire to deflate unsuitable pretension. Frances Ross Galloway recognized in the nun some familiarity with the importance of nomenclature, some willingness to accept that a child might have status.

'That's just because Daddy's grandmother was a Ross,' Elizabeth pronounced when Louise tried to wonder why Frances kept on about it.

'It was Mammy kept on giving her the full name, I think she thought Daddy would like it. Not like us.'

No, the two eldest had been named to reflect the English lines; when they were older the girls were to ponder this – after all the marriage had been made in haste. Why call up the opposition in naming the offspring?

Again it was Elizabeth who came close to an answer then:

'He just had an eye out for the main chance. He must have thought Mammy was well-connected. The names do sound rather grand. Perhaps she told him lies.'

'Perhaps she told him the truth, and he didn't believe her.' Louise by then had no memory of her mother, and

14

had created a comfortingly beautiful, truthful, mis-understood being to take her place.

These were the mysteries of their lives. Elizabeth was the one to pronounce on them, for she was the eldest, and she was the one who had had the adventure.

Although not comfortable, the convent was clean and warm. Set on a slight eminence halfway along the street of a village, it had not been remote, but remained sternly untouched by the life which wavered around the gates. The school also took in day-girls from the immediate area, but most of its pupils were boarders, children of strong farmers and the less ambitious pro-fessionals. The nuns were of the same stock as the pupils, sturdy, unimaginative, devout.

The little Galloway girls were immediately recognized as not the same.

'Protestant,' whispered one of the prefects gathered in council around the Head Girl. 'A mixed marriage!' the others breathed back, their eyes brighter for this vision of a sin so mortal as to be beyond their wildest imaginings. The Head Girl resisted the romance; the girls were baptized Catholics, it was just that their mother had been English. And—as she dropped her voice the others crouched closer to hear the wonder-ful words – 'And—the mother ran away! Left her husband!'

Who had told them this? Not the people who told Elizabeth, for no one told Elizabeth. There had been a furious bustle in the cottage near Kilkenny town, her mother preparing for the return of their father just before Christmas. Rubbish was burned, bags and news-papers and magazines and even old clothes and shoes. Louise and Fanny were given the job of touring the neighbourhood, as far as their small feet would carry them, with a box filled with seven kittens, the rival litters of two cats, in order to find homes for them.

Two shopkeepers had taken an animal each; the little Galloway girls were liked in the town, and when people talked of them it seemed as if their mother was included

15

in the appellation. The children trudged to the mill, where the cashier took one out of pity for them, asking her brother to drown it when she got it home. Some of the men gathered around them, their hands floury cradles for the kittens, assessing them with kind jokes. Three more were taken. The girls knew they would be safe there, would grow fat on rats and milk. But they were left with one. Fanny began to cry, she was so tired and so weighted with this final responsibility. Louise declared that she didn't care, she was too hungry and her feet were sore and she was going home with the kitten, no matter what their father might say.

In the cold dusk they tried to run, but the kitten kept slipping from their arms as they took turns in carrying it, and finally Louise dropped it altogether so that it scampered away into the weeds by the river-bank and what with tears and the dim light and the damp on the grasses they could neither find it nor decide where to look. Fanny said and said ever afterwards that she could hear it crying, but Louise insisted that it was gone and that it would find somewhere safe for itself until the morning and that Mammy would murder them if they didn't get home, it must be very late.

There were lights on in all the rooms so that the cottage looked larger than it ever seemed to the children, who lived most of the time in the kitchen and shared only one of the bedrooms. Elizabeth was carrying a box of bottles out to the shed, and Mrs Galloway, sitting at the kitchen table writing out a list, only glanced at the girls and told them there was a pan of fried potatoes in the range for their supper. She never asked why Fanny was crying, and she never asked them about the kittens. And they never told her.

The floor of the kitchen was flagged with smooth stones on which pretty rugs were thrown. The furniture was big, old and battered, but there was a softness to it appreciated by both people and cats, and here and there on the painted walls hung pictures brought back by Mr Galloway from London, and in the corners huge pottery jars, made in the surprising sheds of Englishmen living in the county, were full of dried rushes the children gathered, and bunches of preserved flowers Mr Galloway brought from Paris. While the two younger girls were out, the range had been blacked and the dresser dusted, the floors swept throughout the long cold passage linking the rooms. Holly from the tree in the garden was laid along the windowsills and over the mantel-shelf, and a few early Christmas cards gaily straddled a string across the back door.

Elizabeth bent and lifted over the rubble piled on the floor, and the cards shifted in the light chill breeze that floated through every time she took another bundle out to the shed. Mrs Galloway finished writing; she owed a total of £117 and 14 shillings to the shop-keepers of the town, and wondered how it had happened, what he would say. Getting up, she twisted the piece of paper and thrust in into the fire, adding to the sudden blaze the brown envelope for the parish dues, the accumulated and by now threatening notes from the school, the postcard in a masculine hand with a date and a place and a time written on it and nothing else.

Now she should wash the girls' hair and dry off their good clothes before the fire so they would be presentable when he came the next day. She looked at them, Elizabeth sitting at her supper where Loulou and Fanny had finished. Three pairs of brown eyes looked solemnly back at her, three white faces spoke of exhaustion and anxiety.

They looked foreign to her, as alien as everything in this town had been since her husband selected the picturesque cottage as the home for them until he could live in Ireland permanently and find a larger place. Would that day ever come? She didn't ask whether she wanted it to; life had an inevitability for her, its phases dictated by the will of other people. But these three little people were her own, as it struck her now.

'You're great girls. But we're all too tired now to do any more. I'm sure everything will be all right. Let's go

17

to bed. And let's have a treat: you can all jump in with me, just for tonight. We'll keep each other warm.'

Elizabeth remembered that as a treat, all tucked up together in the big brass bed, bigger and brassier as she remembered, but indeed it had been big enough for the four slender bodies. Louise did not remember it at all but thought she did, lace-hung and with a canopy. Frances dreamed all through her life afterwards, when her dreams were happy, that she was alseep in someone's arms, but she could never tell whose arms they were.

Sr Perpetua put her arms around her, once. The nun had only been a postulant then, of course. Still called Sr Margaret Rose. Her mother, Mother Benignus decided, must have been mad out of her mind over royalty, and she insisted that until her Profession the young aspirant would be called only Sr Margaret. But Sr Margaret had confided in Frances as she held the child on her lap. They sat in the huge, bright kitchen, every scoured pan and plate put away in the painted caverns of cupboards. She had found Frances at the Marian grotto, crying as she tried to reach one of the convent kittens which had trapped itself on the highest stones. The child wanted to rescue the little animal, but also she wanted to hold it, to feel it, to feel through it some trace of a familiar atmosphere, of something before the convent.

The postulant was an agile girl, the youngest child in a family of four older brothers. The kitten's wails and the little girl's gasping pleas spurred her to undignified action as she kilted her black skirt and jumped first and then climbed the bulging stone. To Frances' shocked eyes she was going away from the kitten, but Sr Margaret Rose knew a thing or two about frightened cats and climbed above it in order to reach down and grasp it firmly around the neck.

'Picture that!' Sr Margaret Rose laughed when she got to the ground again, handing the spitting bundle of fur to Frances. 'She scratched me. Picture!' She held out the thin seam across the palm of her hand, the translucent skin threaded with red berries. Frances began to sob again, the kitten had escaped her frenzied clutch, and the nun promised her it would find its way to the kitchens without their help. She had to go and wash her hand; would Frances come?

All the smells of all the dinners the girls would ever have in that school welcomed them to the chilly domesticity of the institution, but it was there none the less that Frances found a perch, and even when Sr Margaret Rose had become Sr Perpetua and a figure of some assumed authority the child sensed from her an aura of furtive comfort. Both Louise and Elizabeth shared that suspicion – that with Sr Perpetua there would be some slackening of the rule that the little Galloway girls were to be shown no special favour because of their youth, or their abandonment to the convent.

It was Sr Perpetua who obtained from her own sister-in-law the length of netted veil and the tiara of white satin roses for Frances, to soften the blunt wool ordered by Mother Benignus and paid for by Mr Galloway for her First Holy Communion.

There were other feast-days; with the other girls the little Galloways were confirmed in their religion, attended the annual school concert for parents and dignitaries of the parish, sang at the Mass celebrating the transformation of Sr Margaret Rose into Sr Perpetua, and mourned easily with the rest of the school when an old nun died.

Now Sr Perpetua wore the harsh white headband and black veil of the other sisters. Her brown curls were hidden forever, and her hands were carried out of sight within the folded sleeves of the habit. Yet she was still the leaven in the hard bread of the children's existence, the adult to whom they referred for ease or comfort or explanation.

'She was a good nun!' Louise protested years later.

'It was easy to be good, if you were a nun at all,' retorted Elizabeth. 'But they had such a queer way of showing their goodness, and she wasn't any different, really. She kept the same rules, the same way of looking at things, as they did.'

'No.' Louise was able to insist. 'Perpetua was different. She was good because she was holy, really holy. And that made her kinder.'

'She was – *inspired*,' said Frances who was to remember all her life the yellow soap smell from Sr Perpetua's bodice. Choosing her word carefully, she repeated: 'Inspired. She was given the grace to see that the other nuns were right. *We were* different; we upset them. But she was happy in her life so she couldn't be upset, and so she could afford to think about us. I think that's inspiration.'

Elizabeth and Louise looked at her. She was saying the kind of thing that Louise liked to hear, but to Elizabeth her words were a reminder of the way in which Frances could mull over the experiences of her life and produce them as something deeper, more important, different.

'None of those women were inspired. They didn't know the meaning of the word – if they did they couldn't possibly have lived as they did, in that convent, with those weak forbidding priests telling them what to think, and all their lives concentrating on learning their own rules and shoving them into the children they were supposed to be minding.'

Frances smiled: 'Not minding us, Elizabeth. Educating us.'

Louise was still anxious. 'But they entered because something urged them, they had an idea of a life of work and prayer. And sacrifice. Didn't they?'

'Sacrifice?' Elizabeth was scornful. 'What sacrifice? What were they giving up? What did they have to be renounced, to be laid at the altar?'

'Opportunities?' offered Louise.

'They wouldn't know what to do with opportunities,' said Elizabeth, who did.

They had been in the convent for two incredible weeks when she first noticed, at a wicket gate leading into the town's street, a dark-coated woman standing still in the doorway of a shop opposite. Although it was February, and cold, the woman wore no gloves, and her very long, very pale fingers clutched a hand-bag which Elizabeth recognized, a glowing square of red leather inlaid with tapestry panels of golden threads.

'Mammy!' she screamed, and her ecstatic cry sounded out so loud that the woman withdrew immediately into the shadow of the door where other people were going in and out and someone briefly stopped to look around.

Elizabeth ran to the railings, to the wicket; she rattled it but it was locked. Hot desperate tears flooded her throat but when she looked across the road again the woman was outside the shop and laid a white finger against her lips, looking at Elizabeth as she did so. The child quietened at once and stood still.

Her mother walked carefully across the road. Her face was set, dead. A fringe of her black hair flopped from her headscarf, blues and reds and yellows that the girls had loved in a length of shimmering silk.

'Hide them!' She pushed a bag of brown paper through the iron spokes. 'I'll come again soon—' But the child interrupted her.

'Take us home, Mammy! Take us home. We'll be good, we'll go to school. We'll go to Mass; Fanny hasn't stopped asking when are we going home. Tell Daddy we'll be good—'

'Hush!' Her mother's word was fierce and sharp. 'I'll try to come again. You must stay where you are. My darling. My darlings. I'm sorry.' She turned away, and Elizabeth howled as she watched her mother becoming a woman in a dark coat walking away from her, leaving her behind.

This was what made Elizabeth furtive.

'Secretive,' Mother Benignus announced, at last, finding the true word to describe the escaped personality of the child who was never detected in actual wrong-doing.

Not like Frances, hauled in screams of tears from class because she would persist in saying *ay* instead of

21

ah, shall instead of *will*, all the Anglicizations the nuns abhorred. To Frances these were like threads to a web, membership of the mesh of the world beyond the convent walls, beyond which she rarely went.

The brown bags brought by Elizabeth from a place she would not divulge were not threads, but claws. The buns inside them, stale but sticky, had a taste which hurt her heart. For a while, like Elizabeth, she had found a perch on the old stone wall of the convent's flower-garden from where she could see the green dust announcing the daily bus and for a while she thought she would wait, but it grew cold, and she did not know what it was she awaited, and one day there was something else to do. But she held on still to those things that made her different, so that when the other girls in her class, in her dormitory, reminded one another that they must not have too much to do with the Galloways they all understood that there was, indeed, some reason even if they could not tell what it was.

These years for the three girls were not all barren. There were school outings; there were games, a rough scramble with hurley-sticks after a small stitched ball with a vicious bite to the hand or the face; there were concerts. There were occasional friendlinesses from among the students, for they were not the only misfits and other, rescuing parents came and took them out to tea, or to the cinema.

There were visits from their father. On the first of these the girls were too frightened to ask him about their mother. All he represented to them was some earlier hint of guilt, a reason for hiding things, for hiding themselves. The sound of him was the sound of a storm in the night which blew their home away and banished their mother, the noise of loud hard words which made Mrs Craig, from the Rectory, apologize stiffly for interfering, but . . . With terrified eyes they saw her blush and turn back to the bright green gate between the holly trees, the berries no redder than her mortified face.

When the black car drew up so close to the gate that its door opened into the gap they entered it as though they were entering a tunnel of shame, and it was not until days later in the convent, when Louise discovered that she was to wear a nightdress in the bath, that humiliation broke in and grief and loneliness and bewilderment clattered and sprawled and beat at her in great wet clouts. Elizabeth too had wept but quietly, she would not let them see, but Frances had torn off the small shift in a rage and stepped into the bath threatening to bite anyone who tried to put it back on her. The scandal of that episode lingered for the rest of the school, but no one but the nuns knew that to the end of her days in the convent Frances was the only child to bathe alone and naked.

'It will seem strange to you for a while,' their father said. 'You will find it hard at first. But you will be staying here until you finish school, and it will be up to you to make it pleasant or unpleasant, depending on your behaviour.'

Elizabeth said nothing, but Louise, sobbing gently, reminded their father of his wife who had trembled her way into his affection. She had been such a sweet little thing, after all, and so delighted with his praise, so eager for his company. Although she had a Bible – a family Bible, she had called it – the religion thing did not seem to mean very much to her as she never went to church when he knew her first. It was in the family Bible that he read the names, Grace Holderness from her loving mother Elizabeth Gascoyne Holderness, and asked her about them and discovered the landed, newly landless Gascoynes not so far back at all. How would her family, her families, react if she married a Catholic, if she turned, as turn she must? He did not see that the questions meant nothing to her, there were no Gascoynes in her life, her mother was long dead and no one had come from the Holdernesses to relieve her of her meagre office job and spin her away to the Hall and its stables and shooting-parties and church pew. She

23

had changed eagerly, confirming herself in his love, marrying quickly, quietly, depending on his sustenance.

'Your mother has gone back to live in England,' he told them. Elizabeth could tell he was lying, looking at his teeth under his black moustache. She was the one who had heard him lie before, before their mother ceased to appease him. She had watched how those many welcomes after his journeys abroad had melted before his discomfort, his haste to be ready for another trip. She had known he was ashamed of them when they all went to Mass together, and Fr Smayle had said, 'You're getting to be quite a stranger, Mrs Galloway,' in that way he had that meant something else, and their father had said wasn't there anything else to put on the girls except the red hand-knitted jerseys which he said, accurately if he meant robins, made them look like birds.

Was it after that lie that Frances stopped looking for the bus with her mother in it? Elizabeth did not know, and never told the other two of her fearful, shameful vigil at the wicket gate in the convent railings, but told them for the years after that they needed to hear it how their mother loved them. Really. How nothing had been her fault – and that was another lie.

'Of course you will miss your mother,' Mr Galloway allowed as he drove them to a restaurant in another town. 'But she is not able to look after you now that you are growing so big. You need to be at school. She could not manage the money and you were not being properly dressed, or properly educated. You never went to Mass.'

'We went to Church.' Frances, before Elizabeth could stop her, wanted to put him right. 'We did, Daddy. We went to Mr Craig and I was at Sunday School. I know a lot about the Bible now – I was good.' She thought she could appease him too, and tried, and Louise, trying like the others to be terrifically well-behaved, told him politely that in Mr Craig's churchyard they had found a head-stone with Galloway on it.

'Madeline Gwendolyn Galloway,' recited Louise in her remembering voice. 'Born April 1885, died August 1893: *For he shall give his angels charge over thee, to keep thee in all thy ways.*'

'That's a Protestant church, and you're not Protestants.' Mr Galloway hit on the truth at last. 'You're Catholics, and from now on you're going to a Catholic school and a Catholic Church, and you'll be brought up by right-thinking women who know the difference between right and wrong and who know the meaning of sacraments and vows and who'll train you to be good wives and mothers too.'

His vehemence was too much for Frances, who began to cry: 'I want *my* wife and mother. She's *my* wife and mother too,' and Louise sat silent beside her, her eyes hunting the pastures outside the car, the fields foaming with daisies.

'Will Mammy come and visit us?' asked Elizabeth, who knew she would make her mother take them all home.

'I don't know,' the answer was quick. 'That's up to her.' But he did know how little of what was up to her Mrs Galloway was capable of doing.

Louise must have understood him, somehow. Once when Elizabeth had grown tired of watching for the green bus, she saw Louise climbing the wall and sitting on the one smooth stone.

'What are you looking out for?' Elizabeth was surprised. She had never seen Louise here before.

'Oh, nothing,' Louise said, straightening her serge skirt over her knees. 'I just thought it's been a while since Daddy came. He might come today. Perhaps I'll see his car on the road.'

'Don't catch cold,' warned Elizabeth, leaving a vigil she would not keep, and indeed Louise did not keep it for long that day, or ever again.

They were not the only girls staying on in the convent when the school-terms ended, although Mother Benignus often advised other parents against letting

25

their children remain during the holidays because they would have the company only of the Galloway girls. But before Sr Margaret Rose became Sr Perpetua the nun was allowed a last visit home and as it was summer-time she asked if Frances might be allowed to accompany her.

The yellow farmhouse held on to a slope of foothill, with small fields spraying out from the yards in front and behind. A brief level patch of land at the side of the steep house had been given over to an orchard where apples grew with blackcurrants and loganberries, and all the south facing windows in the house had their inside ledges studded with ripening tomatoes. There had been too many children in that household for Frances to be made a stranger; the girl of the moment was Margaret Rose, and around her a complex drama began to weave as soon as she got out of the bus in the village and into her father's trap, the only conveyance of the kind Frances had ever seen and which was one of the many uncomplicated delights of her visit.

It was the time for making hay, but Margaret Rose had no work of that kind to do, staying instead in the kitchen by day to make the cakes, to cook the huge hams and coils of cold grey beef which emerged, glistening and red and pungent with salt from the huge pans on the range. When the boys and their father came in they brought other men, and in the long evenings they sat indoors and out, and the air filled with pipe and cigarette smoke and the girls and women from other farms, from the village, came up to talk and to drink stout and sherry and port and later, when most of the women were gone, the unnamed white liquid that made people gasp and swear.

Frances fitted into this life like a drop of water into a well. She slept in a truckle bed and rose with the first light, lingering in her room only to savour the adult delight of being alone. In the kitchen she was allowed to turn her hand to anything that came her way, frying the thick chunks of bread for the early breakfasts or making up a feed for the hens, to every one of which she had given a name within a day of seeing them. She picked fruit in the orchard, and topped and tailed the yellow and red gooseberries while sitting on the wall of flat stones outside the house. The father and brothers of Margaret Rose were quiet, undemonstrative men, but one of them – afterwards she always insisted to herself that his name was Thady – had shyly brought her a piece of honeycomb, its golden juice running among the dark green bubbles of a cabbage leaf. At noon she carried baskets with Margaret Rose down to the groups of men in the fields, napkins covering piles of bread and meat, scones pitted with currants, cans of steaming tea, tall tin jugs of milk, and in the evening when the pale deal table in the kitchen was dressed with the hams, the chickens, the bowls as big as cradles of potatoes, it was her task to stand on the wall beyond the front door and wave a white tablecloth so that they would all come home together. Margaret Rose's mother presided at these feasts with the same genial calm she beamed when standing over the washtub or directing the plunging streams of milk from the patient cows in the byre. Frances had had a feeling that there was something rude about this intimate contact with the animal teat, but when she tried it herself and felt the silk skin yield to her grasp and the milky stream begin to flow, she flushed with the pleasure of success and discovered innocent sensuality.

The entire family went to Mass together, the women making the journey in the trap pulled by the vigorous brown pony Frances had learned to pet. There were many ponies and carts at the church gates, a few round cars as well, and inside, the cool church sweated with people aching to be out of doors once more. The priest was small and fat and hot and tossed Latin on the marble altar alight with flowers and candles, and preached a sermon about the foreign missions as quickly as he could. Fasting from the night before and now accustomed to a hearty breakfast Frances felt thin with hunger when she went to the altar-rails with Margaret Rose. While the host melted on her tongue her thoughts were all of sausages and tomatoes and the bread and gooseberry jam there would be later on; as they left the church in a crowd, one of the boys – it must have been Thady, Frances always said later – pushed a hard square of chocolate into her hand and told her in a whisper to eat it quick before the others would want a bit.

Was it that night, a Sunday night, that was Margaret Rose's last night at home? Forever? The carts and cars came toiling to the front yard, and girls in hard bright clothes with careful hair brought whispered stories to an end when they saw the men coming up. Old women sat in the cool parlour, always known as 'the room' and sipped sherry and were often silent, but the men filled the kitchen and flowed out, young and old, to the airy yard where the girls began to leave their clutter around Margaret Rose and talked lightly about going for a little walk, the evening was so fine. As the couples strayed away and back and changed their partners, a fiddle was brought out and the laments of the valley were offered to the night.

The square swept yard and the flagged kitchen left room for jigs and reels from the old men whose polished boots twisted upon each other as they stepped it out, and the girls and boys whopped through the circles of the set dances, 'The Walls of Limerick', *Casadh an tSúgan*. The sweet wild violin rested while an accordion gave waltzes and a reason, even in front of the hot little priest who had walked up on his own, for the young people to touch one another, to hold and cling and confide in the dying light of the day.

Margaret Rose waltzed too, her brothers and cousins swirling her in their arms, but she grew quiet after just a few dances and sat closer to her mother and father, and to Frances who had moved from wall to door, to window-sill, watching, marking, making it all her own. The mother's face had seemed to Frances to be thinner in these past days, she had been more silent. Frances saw the father's skin burn deeper, not just with the sun, with the reddening that had made his eyes look wet and his mouth tucked in more firmly.

A light boyish tenor carried a tune in from the yard:

'From this valley they say you are going,
We shall miss your bright eyes and sweet smile,
For they say you are taking the sunshine
That brightened our pathways a while.'

A net of voices lifted the song, young voices, the old farmers and villagers and their wives were silent, this was not how they would sing:

'Come and sit by my side if you love me,
Do not hasten to bide me adieu
But remember the Red River Valley,
And the cowboy who loved you so true.'

Louise sang often in the convent, one result of a decision taken, now that the girls were getting older and really *quite* well-behaved, to let them visit the nuns' holiday house in Ardmore.

'Picture!' Sr Perpetua said when Elizabeth told her of the plan.

'You'll be able to swim there, on the nuns' beach: I'll ask Reverend Mother about bathing costumes for you all.'

The square grey house held wonders for them, not least that of seeing nuns from other houses of the sisterhood, not least from watching them at their idea of fun, the more daring producing surreptitious packs of cards, the more kind inviting the girls to join in games of Lotto and Ludo. Their yellow stretch of sand lay with its back to the curve of cardboard dwellings which daily issued streamers of loud-voiced frantic children. Encouraged to ignore all that billowing, bellowing activity the three girls walked instead among the stone cottages of the village, the painted houses terracing the hill above the exciting sea. The nuns had a boat and a boatman and one evening they rowed up to Monatrea on the narrowing Blackwater, the crowded cloudy woods darkening as they returned, the river smell giving way to the tang of the open sea whose waves drove in on them as the little boat lifted on the swell.

Lulled as they had been by their exploration of the old Abbey ruins, nuns and children alike had drifted into an easy silence on the journey home, but now the choppy tilt of the vessel roused them, the shores laden with drowsy trees faded away from the nimbus of the widening bay. The ocean lay before them, and Elizabeth looked again at the slide of water in the bottom of the boat, measuring. The soft little nun from County Meath who had been teaching the girls to swim began to sing – 'Speed, bonny boat, like a bird on the wing' – and the other nuns joined in, the lurching rhythm catching the pull of the oars against the tide. Hearing the words, finding the lilt, Louise blended her voice with the singing voices and left the chorale to raise the song in a harmony of her own, offering a gliding flock of notes to the sudden, smiling stars. The squat lighthouse at Youghal beamed out as the boat crunched on their beach, and even the nuns who could not sing sang as the boatman, his own voice laughing in the night, helped them to jump over the rippled waves that lay against the shore.

Sr Perpetua said she was amazed when Louise told her about joining the school choir. Sr Mary Columbanus had said she was good enough, and her father had been asked to allow a new uniform for the public concert in the hall.

'Picture!' Elizabeth and Frances had said together, folding themselves in giggles and satire, as Louise paraded her new ribbons, perched like grosgrain butterflies on either side of her rosy, satisfied face. Sr Perpetua struggled with the unruly hair which would not stay restrained into plaits, and the unaccustomed children did not recognize the pride in her gaze when she looked at Louise in her finery of serge and poplin.

30

There must have been some tremor of pride, too, in Mr Galloway, for he sent them money for the first time.

'Money each?' wondered Frances, looking at the green notes in Elizabeth's hand.

'Money each,' Elizabeth said, not telling them how much, giving a single pound to Frances, a pound and ten shillings to Louise, keeping two pounds and ten shillings for herself.

'It's for the concert,' Elizabeth explained. 'For the stalls and sweets and things. You can buy what you like.'

It was a Saturday, a brisk winter morning with the school thumping with battened excitement, a feeling of hurried informality, of freedom. On the bus taking her to Mallow, and then on to Cork, Elizabeth breathed a cold consciousness of what she was doing; not running away, running towards. Finding. Answering that letter which spoke of Alton's Shop, South Terrace, care of. Underneath the chill of the adventure ran the hot current of desperation which had cooled into her intention, and hardened. Already skilful at subterfuge it had not been difficult to leave the school, to make herself inconspicuous on the bus, the right bus too.

The mist from the frosted fields yielded to the sunlight as the journey went on, the country outside the windows glistened as if new. The morning sky looked thin and pink as if it had been peeled, and the woods around Blarney floated in brown and purple clouds above the town, the great square keep of the castle standing bare to Elizabeth's searching eyes. The twisting road unrolled towards the city, heralded by sea-gulls and steeples, and at the terminus Elizabeth was baffled by bridges. She asked her way; there was nothing to remark in her teenage demeanour, her queries gave no hint of anxiety, she was shown her route without comment.

Benign everywhere else, at the South Terrace the sun turned ugly. Gaunt houses with small-windowed attics peering from their roofs stood hard on the uneven pavements, and the stepped white planks from the timberyard looked raw against the walls. Alton's shop hid around a corner, its window forlorn with forgotten notices, and inside there was the thick compound smell of cheese and yellow cakes and coal-dust and paraffin. A fat man with a loose lower lip glowered at Elizabeth's question.

'Mrs Galloway? Know her, do ye? We haven't seen her here – and we'd like to, we'd like to. Tell her that – Johnny Alton'd like to see her.'

To see him, purple faced and repulsive, spitting contempt for her mother, was the first shock of this journey for Elizabeth. In the street again she looked wildly around, disoriented and afraid. In her pocket she had enough money to get back to the school if she had to go back, that was not her fear. What gripped her was the loneliness of her concentration; what if the centre of her heart were not to be found? It was almost a year since she had last seen her mother, there had been months between each stolen meeting, encounters with no joy offering nothing except continuity, a link with what had once been her life, their lives. This search assumed that the continuity was rooted, that her mother came to Elizabeth from a place in which their lives could thrive again. It was hope, no more; now Elizabeth faced despair.

Cracked steps led to an open door, gaping into a littered, cavernous hall. By asking and asking Elizabeth had found a possible person; maybe her mother was the English lady in number 16. Her second thumping knock on the door, the lead knocker falling heavily from her hand to the peeling timber, produced a voice at least, and that voice high and uncertain and known.

The woman with greying hair looked at the girl.

'Elizabeth?' There were no outstretched arms, no tears of joy, 'What in the name of God are you doing here? You must go back, go back at once!'

The hall echoed to her voice, the startled words

glancing off the stairs and ceiling. Elizabeth had expected surprise but no anger, and she heard anger in the echoes. The elation of her success vanished. She became very young again, she could not speak.

'Oh God, what am I to do with you now? You must go back, you must!'

A call, thick and male, came through the vault of the stairs: 'Lally? What are you doing down there? What's going on?'

Mrs Galloway looked at Elizabeth sadly. The girl had shivered as she heard the shouted name. Lally. Her mother's pet name. She had no memory, now, of her father ever using it. It had been theirs, held between the mother and her daughters, theirs only.

'You'd better come up. It's freezing here.'

Climbing the stairs after her, Elizabeth saw how the trousers fell like bags from her mother's bones. The grimy light falling through the landings as they mounted showed her face older, worn, without the flush of secrecy. Her hair was still long, but falling from its metal grips at the back and almost colourless, its blackness faded and wan, its dull fringe stranded with grey. Elizabeth had no sense of her own self; no idea of how, to her mother, she looked tall and firm with health, bright with the colours of youth. Cared for, if not cared about.

A strong bewitching smell met Elizabeth; in a cluttered room a fire burned eagerly, and the man standing by the hearth, a glass frothing in his hand, was laughing as he looked at her.

'Who's this, then? One of your sprats?'

Through his beard his lips were very red.

'This is our all, young lady. We've no place to put you – unless you want to squeeze between Lally and me on the bed?'

It was a joke, but a brutal one to the girl. She had seen the brass bed with its tumbled coloured covers, the man's clothes on the hook on the wall. The window had no curtains, and beside its light an easel stood firm,

33

a table nearby held tubes and pots, brushes stood on end with pencils and black sticks, there were hues and textures everywhere, fabric, substance. Only Mrs Galloway looked bleached.

'What will I do with her? She's run away from school.'

'Send her back. There's nothing else for it. Pity and all that, Lally, but she can't stay here.'

It was happening to Elizabeth. It was happening, as it had happened before, but this time she had invited it. She was dumb with the disaster.

Drinking his beer, the man explained.

'Couldn't keep you even if we had the room. We're packing up here, going off. To England, where I can sell my work. Art has no place in Ireland, these days – ever get out of that convent of yours, to a museum, a gallery? Of course not!'

He was not indignant. Elizabeth thought through his words to the pink and white plaster statue of the Virgin in the school hall, the great bleeding crucifix in the church, the Stations of the Cross.

'We have a lot of statues and pictures,' she said at last, stung to defence. 'And we have art. Art classes. Sr Bonaventure takes us for art and physical education.'

'Oh, that's it all right, art and physical education.' The sneer went out of his tone: 'Like it, do you? The school? Like being with your sisters?'

Elizabeth could not tell him of her need. She could not tell either how she knew about the passage of time, that for her before too long there would be decisions, departures, a life after school.

To her silence he said: 'Better to stick it out. Education always has a price on it, and at the end of this you'll be educated. That's a lot, you know. And in the meantime – food, shelter, clothing, company; is it so bad? What more could anyone want?'

Mrs Galloway handed him another bottle of beer and Elizabeth looked at him, the cold light trembling as it warmed by the fire, how he stood in it at ease, his life around him but portable, the woman waiting.

'My mother,' she began, unconsciously talking to him, as if Mrs Galloway were not there. The woman moved from her stand by the fire, uneasy.

'I came to see my mother. That's all. We had a free day at school and I had the money so I came to see her. I'm going back on the next bus. It is all right.'

Something from her tight distress must have reached Mrs Galloway. She took coins from a plate on the mantelpiece.

'Here – a few bob for the trip. Button your coat up now, it's so cold. I'll walk to the bus with you, and you can tell me about the girls.'

In the street Mrs Galloway said: 'He looked after me, Elizabeth, when I was in trouble. You can't know about all the things that have happened to me. Try not to think badly of me. Please.'

'It's all right,' Elizabeth said politely. 'I only came to see you. I thought, when I leave school, I should know where you live. That's all. It's all right.'

They waited in a long silence for the bus, sitting in the shabby terminus in the comfortless cold. People shuffled around them, herded between tannoy and notice-board. Poor people, country people, with sacking bags spilling intimacies.

Squalid, Elizabeth realized. This is squalid, it is sordid, this whole place, this whole thing. Her mother too. *'Lally!'* she said fiercely to herself. *'Lally!'* and her fury broke into anguish and Lally sitting beside her saw tears spout from her daughter's desperate eyes.

'I'll have to go now,' she whispered sharply. 'Stop crying, nothing is any worse than it was.'

Elizabeth's sobs were loud, helpless.

'Stop it.' Mrs Galloway had risen. 'Please, darling, do stop it. I must go, people are looking at us. Don't worry about me, I'll be all right. Oh, do stop crying, Elizabeth. Goodbye. I have to go – I *must!*'

People thought the girl was distressed at parting, and explained her tears kindly to one another. They shepherded Elizabeth onto the bus, and at each halt on the long final journey there were gentle words and reminders, a knowing generous feeling for the disablement of grief.

Dark came down on the country like a blanket falling slowly on flame, and Elizabeth saw through drying eyes how the small lights of houses came through the blackness, their chill radiance as distant as the stars. The convent was bright, brimming with sound and life as she fitted herself into the back row of the school hall, among classmates who had noticed her absence without wondering.

She was in time for the choir, Louise's choir; they sang in Irish the song about Kilcash, the lament for a life that was lost, the house and its lady no more. '*Cad a dheanfaimid feasta gan adhmad*?' What shall we do for timber now, the last of the woods have fallen? What shall we do for timber, Elizabeth thought, searching for shelter from the loss of her life.

Frances found her.

'We knew you were gone. We didn't tell anyone. Only Sr Perpetua, because she came looking for you at tea-time. But Louise told a lie, and it's all right. Where were you? Where did you go?'

With her money she had bought a book about an English boarding school – *Dimsie*; apples and sweets and a lace-edged handkerchief of white cotton with a satin rose in the corner, an E for Elizabeth stitched around the flower.

'It's for you. E for Elizabeth. I was thinking of you. Where did you go to?'

Louise too had thought of Elizabeth, lying quickly and efficiently when required, although perhaps Sr Perpetua had not believed her.

'But she's such a pet she won't tell, not now you've come back. Where did you go?'

'I went to Cork.' Elizabeth saw their eyes round, their mouths open. 'I thought I knew where Mummy would be.'

There was a luminosity in their faces. They loved this

adult Elizabeth, who was daring, and brave on their behalf. They shone with excited hope.

Elizabeth shook her head.

'No. She wasn't there. I thought I knew, but I tried there and they said she was gone. Gone to England. And then I came home.'

Although the hope was gone, the excitement was still there, the energy of the adventure. Frances wanted more, the details, the bus, the people, the shops. She would live on it for months. Louise saw some outline of a disaster, but said only, 'So, Daddy was right. Remember, he told us she was gone back to England.'

'Oh, yes,' Elizabeth agreed. 'Daddy was right.'

The years after that explained many of the mysteries to the girls, although not in order, or in due time. Where there were no explanations, understanding came instead, slowly.

'Perhaps it would have been better if we had been boys – better for Daddy, I mean,' pondered Frances. After his funeral Elizabeth had left her teacher-training college to deal with solicitors, her first object being the release of her sisters from the convent. It had puzzled and hurt her that they did not want to go, not before time.

'Still, he left us all he had,' said Louise, who at last was learning to be a singer. 'He must have wanted to do that, wanted us to have what he had, whether we were boys or girls. Boys might have satisfied his pride or something, but he would still have had to do something about us, or them, you know what I mean. I mean, there would still have been a problem.'

'Anyway,' Elizabeth said, always the pragmatist, 'he didn't have any choice in the matter. We were all he had, so he had to leave it to us. We were his heirs.'

'Heiresses,' corrected Frances at last at University.

'Heiresses,' said Elizabeth, not thinking at all of the room in Cork with its smell of turpentine, its brass bed.

'And I will never understand why he hated us.' Frances had decided that he did, a long time ago.

'What I will never understand,' said Elizabeth, 'is why *they* hated us. The nuns.'

'Ah, they didn't all hate us,' said Louise, thinking of the glory of music. 'Not Sr Mary Columbanus; she taught me to sing, she liked to hear me singing. I think she liked me.'

'And not Sr Perpetua,' said Frances, looking at the newspaper with Lady Elizabeth Holderness and the Gascoyne Trophy. 'Not Sr Perpetua.' And her fingers lightly outlined the shape and shadows of the picture.

Just Fine

'And how are you, yourself?' he asked.

The question was so unexpected that she blushed. Heat rushed through her and she turned her head towards the street, looking blindly through the grey window of the solicitor's office where they both sat in a calm of waiting, agreed on settlement, terms, undertakings, custodies, maintenance and matrimonial ownership, waiting now only for the formality of documents and signatures.

The question and its implications tipped the balance of silence between them. For Michael it was only a gesture he meant to be able to make, a sign of continuing concern about what might happen to her, how she would manage, how things were working out with the child.

For Martha it was more. Bewildered thoughts battered against each other in her head; what was it he wanted to know? Could she tell him what happened about the income tax? Or would this be the right time to mention the fees for the nursery school, or the fact that the exhaust pipe was loose, yet again, in her car? What was he *asking* her?

The panic in her head sat back into words which she did not speak, but which seemed to hurl themselves from her temples against the window through the glass, onto the street of the city where it seemed to her they bounced and recoiled and rang out again, a sounding of her rage.

'How am I? Myself? Oh, now to be truthful, to be truthful, I am fine. But lonely. Lonely. And different.

That clean word rings clear, like a bell in my mind, different, yes, and glad to be. The new two of us in this long new time have found that there is less and less to be afraid of. I can climb over the rubble of mortgage repayments to find old crocus bulbs sending up their striped shafts of green in the garden. We are not afraid of the icy roads of winter without you, or of the windows rocking in the dark wind. The dark without Daddy is no more than just the dark.

'Look at the bills, the bills are smaller. One fire will do us, there is no threat in the telephone. My bed is my own, unshared, and going to sleep at night is like sliding into friendly water. The house, yes, the house is yours, and like a shell you are welcome to the shape of it, for we are the flesh inside and we thrive. What can I say about our linked lives except this: we are happy together.

'And if I am lonely it is not because the man in my life is only four years old. I am lonely for something I may not have recognized when I had it, if I had it, and which I cannot describe now. The closest I can come is that these words have to stay inside here, in a new place in which I have come to live, but which I now know is not an exile, it is just somewhere else. *Me.*'

When the pattern of hidden words changed and slowed Martha's silence changed too, for with her arrival at herself she had brought one piece of luggage. Her journey had the weight of a ghost strapped to its back, the ghost of a question, what was happening to him?

Where was he living? What would they tell the boy together as their last shared undertaking for him? Oh, this was a question with a deepening range, a query which went on further, touching against corners it could not probe. Martha's greatest fear now was that a disturbance of the secrecy of this man's life might reveal, in its hollows, a space for her. And while there was a need to know something, something that could be told as 'just fine!', perhaps – she did not want to know if a room was being kept for her.

She had already established so firmly in her heart that the child which had been born of the two of them was now forever to be only his or hers, there was no 'theirs', no future fusion which could bind them to anything together ever again. In this savagery of sundering she found passion and strength, hard hot words which made sense to her and put a pattern on chaos. Once, early on, perhaps two years before this meeting of settlements, she had given herself a picture of what was happening to their marriage. She had seen herself, sitting among the ruins, numbering the bricks; Michael did not even notice the collapse.

It was then that she had realized that the boy was a brick also, a part of a structure which she had thought must remain because he was within it. Had she still loved her husband then, when it was technically 'before'? – another unasked question, or at least a silent one, easily postponed. No, something had been happening to her then as well as to him, or rather *with* him, for he had not changed, she thought, nothing had happened 'to' him. For after all, what had happened, the actual occurrence, had only been, again, a question.

'This is our last child, isn't it? Can you see any way in which we will sleep together again, as husband and wife, or have more children?'

His gentle 'no' solidified so that the air in the space between them was a wall of stone. The marriage flung itself against it and broke and died in that instant. The heavy roses on the curtains and the chairs glowed like wreaths; beyond them the garden was laden with autumn, its weighted leaning trees framing the small figure, red-anoraked, a pom-pom hat pulled far down over his ears so that eyes, nose and little pursed mouth made a small intent mask, while the small hands, with rake and brush, sculled the grass to gather and heap the drifting leaves.

The remembered picture came to her complete, and she remembered too how they had been surrounded in that conversation by the comfort they had created together, but which it then seemed they could not touch, fabrics which might blister and split at the pressure of their taut bodies. It was as though the tension had crystallized, as though everything was sharp and shining, cold and hard to the touch if they dared to touch the materials of their disappearing lives.

What had they said at that time that had brought them to this? Had it been just that question and that answer? Of all that went before, the betrayal and all she had been told, Martha found it hard to give herself accurate evidence. It was true, of course, but was it accurate? What had happened, what exactly had been the cause of this effect?

In this blaze of immediate confusion, while Michael's question roiled and broke among the rocky caves of her mind, memory made her want to say only this, to say what were the things she would never say.

'We will never say to you – come back, come back to eat at another table in another room, away from the worry of our noise; come back to read the shorter fairy tale, to give abstracted praise, to listen and not remember, to live a deeper lie.' Unuttered, these alone were the insubstantial slights her heart had listed. But these could not be all. If they were, were they all that was left?

In the office they sat on stiff chairs of ornamented wood and sharp brown leather. Outside, the Mall uncoiled its stream of traffic winding past the Imperial Hotel, down towards the bridges. Against a sky luminous with winter the spires of the Cathedral were pointed with cold. Only minutes had passed in the silence inside, but from the street the evening beat against the brick and stone of these buildings, climbing to its usual crescendo of people pounding homewards.

Michael sat in shadow, but turned his head towards her when she spoke.

'I'm just fine,' Martha said. She looked at him. His face was flushed with tears.

Truth

In the cattle truck the little girl was held by her mother's arms against motherly breasts, her own arms locked around her mother's neck. Crushed by other bodies, their two bodies merged with the train's pace. The child's face was closed in sleep, the mother's was openly showing the exhaustion of terror. Held together they swayed with the other bodies held together and the mother's eyes found among that mass the bodies of her husband and her son. The boy, eight years old, lay against his father's shoulder.

The train ranted on, rattling them into even closer fusion, merging them into one another and into the throng of other terrors rank and sweating about them. They swayed. The boy slept. Unimaginably the father slept also, not real sleep but a standing doze, a daze, as he swung in the tight lurch of the people in the train, in the night.

Slowly the listless body of the boy began to slide, head first, across his father's back from where he had rested against the shoulder. Across the truck, across the standing, moving crush of people, that sloping slide found his mother's eyes. As the child's head disappeared into the black impenetrable pack, moving silently and forever into the waiting maw that gulps soundlessly the little victims of history, as his father, the pawnbroker, awoke to his first consciousness of consuming guilt, the mother opened out her despair and screamed and screamed until her shrieks rang out of the cattle truck and poured themselves in flame along the corridors, breaking open the door of the delivery room, consuming without concern everything that lay in their path back to the mother's mouth.

Peggy traced their vivid trajectory from her bursting uterus with an amazed sense of ownership. Earlier she had cried out only for help, only for someone to stay near, just for a minute; her calls contained apology, a knowledge of weakness, a sad admission of fear of meeting each new change alone. In whole minutes of quiet she did sums of length of contraction, about pethilorfan and pethidine and oxytocia. Was it time, surely it was time, the next one would bring the nurse with an injection, with orders for a release from the drip, for stirrups, for dear familiar words like fully dilated, words and actions to be scattered over her like the largesse of mercy.

Perhaps, it could be, it was time even for them to ring the doctor again, to tell the obstetrician about her. He might not come but surely he would say two cc's, or take her off the drip, and soon after that, surely he would come, and then they would all help her.

She remembered, what was her mind doing to her, she remembered that girl in Galway, the girl who had gone from the delivery table to the window and who was able to jump then and put an end to it all. In spite of them. Here the window was a small one, blue curtained to look homely. It had the advantage, though, of opening out, so that part of it would be easy. The thing would be to get to it, really. Well, she could use the padded chair, the black one, used by that nurse last night, was it last night? Yesterday? That girl who had sat in the room with her, with her back turned, so that you could see the pretty dark curls under the white cap, she had been reading *True Romances*.

It would be easy, from the bed to the chair and then from the chair to the cupboard beneath the window, and she would not mind the tearing pain because she would be doing something to end it. Easy, all that part of it. Easy, the little toppling shove that would launch

44

her down into seething, travelling, trapped bodies that would pack around her, with them she would rock and the train would bear them all on, swaying deeper and deeper into the foreign forests and the screams that were awaiting her and which now would not wait but unleashed themselves again and again and then again through her convulsing body.

The steel lips of the moon in the corner drew back into her husband's smile.

'I'm off, love,' he said. 'You'll be all right. They'll take care of you. I'll get a steak and a pint in the Whiffenpoof, and I'll ring later on.'

Fingers squeezed her pinioned hand and a friendly voice said – 'Goodnight, Mr Sullivan.'

Mr Sullivan? Mr Sullivan? She lifted herself to her elbows to see goodnight Mr Sullivan but he was gone, only the swing of the door left behind him. All that was left with her was the night, no help there, and the moon with its black smiling teeth in the corner, smiling and smiling as the boy's head began its inexorable descent into the waiting dark.

In a panic of pain she drew breath and let it out again on a screeching sound that carried her consciousness beyond her fettered body. In Spain once, she had read about it in a cheap book about the Civil War, a girl on a farm got pregnant when she wasn't married. Her father and brothers waited until she went into labour and then they dragged her into a wood and tied her down and tied her legs together and that was how she died and that was how the baby died.

That's how Aunty Pearl died, she thought. Remember Aunty Pearl. I remember Mam remembering. They brought the blood down in buckets from her bed. That was the upstairs room in the litte white-washed house out there near Inniscarra, near the graveyard, near where the dam is now. Her fourth, that had been, and here they were, all four of them. Padraig, Neilus, Conor and Sean. Oh yes, all four. No Aunty Pearl. Her fourth. My second.

No, the real problem here was going to be releasing herself from the drip. That was going to be squeamishly messy, a little bit of new pain. She could only see the thin tube as it lay against her arm, the entry of the cannula hidden by strapping. Even getting that stuff off would be a bit sickening. But there was the window, the kind small welcoming window, that would make up for the pinch of the needle, the tug of the bandage. It would make up for everything.

What would she do, though, if they came in for something and found her about to climb? They'd send her up to Our Lady's, and who would listen to her there, who would understand that she hadn't wanted to be a trouble to anyone but that someone should have come and helped her? Up there she could wander the corridors forever, in slippers and other people's cardigans, she would lose her own smell and begin to smell like those other women, her hair cut straight and her shoulders rounded with indifference. Would she become like Mrs Sweeney, with her ten children? After each birth Mrs Sweeney was brought for months to Our Lady's, for she thought each nativity was that of the infant Jesus. All the ten children were brought to visit her, smelling of their home in the countryside, by their kind stumbling father who would bring her home and make her pregnant again within weeks.

Or would she, finding herself there, become so determined on oblivion that she would make her way irrevocably to the river avoiding to fool them the high windows and all they offered?

'I'll fool them! I'll fool them!'

Peggy planned her escape even as the truck rattled through landscapes unseen, but she could see now without windows, these were meadows of savage callousness, untouched by her agonized travelling through them.

The motion would not stop. Surely now it was time for someone to come. She was thirsty, drained in every interior crevice, her lips cracked and hurt when she stretched her mouth around a scream. Could they not hear the difference in her cries? She wasn't asking any more for the pain to be taken, all she wanted now was for someone, someone to be with her so that this frightful, unrelenting journey would not be made entirely alone. However it should end, let it not go on alone.

'Oh, frightful,' came her whisper on the antiseptic air. She gasped to be released. Release me, whispered back her mind. Let me out and I will lie under the wheels so that the life can be crushed quickly out of me, yes, I will hold my child in my arms and quietly against my body and let us crush us both together, I can feel the oily dirt of the tracks, their scum on my skin, the bruising cinders will be welcome to me and in the stillness of the hills, the calm air, I will welcome the rushing roar of the train and the crunch of its wheels on my bones so that for me and mine forever the end will come at last.

In a fever of dehydration her mind swam back to the council cottage on the road beyond Carrigaline, where Una was safe with her father, where the flowered curtains at the gable window let in to a small sloping room with the waiting cot, the Beatrix Potter wall frieze. Una must never know what was happening here.

It was strange to Peggy that in this tired moment her seeking eyes could not fix on Una's little face, the shape and texture of it were not discernible. Yet the cottage with its flowered windows was clear in white and green. Clear too were the ferns and pines of the hillside above it, with its ash and laurels and elder and oak. Clear and green and smooth was the deep river that flowed beneath, that part of the river beyond Coolmore which was called a pool and which was always deep, always still, yet flowing softly underneath.

Dark as a mystery the river here; oh how gratefully her mind shone on it now, this river bearing only a few old boats, creaking with red or blue paint flaking with time. Sometimes, in summer, a streamlined yacht sailed up from the busier anchorages at Crosshaven and harboured for a warm month or two, with English voices sounding across the glassy stillness at night, voices floating as the slender craft twisted slowly and gently on the easeful water.

The drenching wet began somewhere behind her head. Wetness from her eyes slid across her nose as she turned again towards the window where the sky showed daybreak. Her gown was wet, the sheet beneath her saturated with water and with sticking blood. There was nothing left in her but those weak tears and pleas and on this second morning all motion had ceased, the pain had changed into an unchanging, incandescent consummation without rhythm, without purpose, without hope.

The green door pushed open on a voice saying – 'Peggy! Mrs Sullivan!'

There was a rush of feet in the corridor outside, hands warming themselves on the still mound of her belly, the glisten of steel on her skin, voices calling hurriedly down the hall, and the telephone ringing. She lay without moving but noted dully an outside difference, a hand on hers, another somehow wiping her mouth with something silky and damp and then the bulk of the big man who was the doctor and who was saying – to her? to someone, 'We had to try it.' And then her whole body was being moved with the murmur of words to console her, to tell her what was happening, around pale green corners on rubber wheels she was being moved, running, into an acre of whiteness and light where another man was waiting with other men and women all busy, all doing things. He came to her side, took her hand, his blue eyes telling her as he pinched and then smoothed the skin of her hand that it was all right, he would look after her, it was all right now.

'Blue eyes,' she thought as she sank. 'Blue eyes! He must surely be Aryan.'

She woke to her own voice: 'and and and and and and . . .' a catalogue of infinity. Here was clarity. Here was a nurse.

'Mrs Sullivan, look, you have a lovely baby boy!'

The bundle with its small black head was tucked inside the flaccid space between her arm and her side. She struggled to fit this new shape into the scene crowding around her.

'Isn't he lovely, Mrs Sullivan, a grand little boy? And so big!'

It was too late. The train was going too fast for her to grip him safely, she could get no purchase on the swaddled body, each lurch of the cattle truck weakened the grip of her hands on the blanket. She saw his black head, the tender curls still damp, she saw it now begin again its aching, inevitable slide down and down into that tiny space, that little opening stretching only to find his little body and swallow him forever.

It was all true. She could not cry out against it, it had happened.

The Swain

'Your swain', her mother had called him. At first it had been gently ironic, there was no sting in it, the older woman had no expectation. And now it was all right. Eileen knew it fitted him, Benny was her swain.

It had nearly not happened. They had left the town within a few years of one another, Benny first as the elder graduate, taking a degree and a boat in the same week and lost for years thereafter to the talk of the town. It was said as easily as these things are said always that his departure had broken his father's heart, but it was more likely that the old man had choked on his avid acres. And then it was said that Benny's irregular marriage – no marriage at all as it turned out – had brought on the stroke. Married in an office abroad in London, with a strap of a one who had already brought down the name of a priest on the island!

As that had been the death of him, Benny's father had no more to fear from further reported irregularities, such as divorce, but the town had anxieties which surfaced when Benny himself arrived home single but not a widower. 'Wiser in their generation', was all the Canon had to say when questioned about the young man's Catholic eligibility. No one knew whether to be relieved or scandalized.

Eileen knew nothing of all this.

'Did I see Benny Cronin in the town today?' she asked her mother as they prepared an evening meal together.

50

'How would I know?' Her mother's approach to life these days was laconic. Her last joy had been Eileen's return after fourteen years in England. Her next delight, in the nature of things, should be the girl's marriage and children, but Mrs Tuohy accepted that these could not be regarded as imminent.

'Well, is he home in Manortreacy, that's all I'm asking? If I knew he was back I'd know whether it was him I saw or not.'

'He's been back working the farm for four years now.' Mrs Tuohy's tone was dry. She had been a poor letter-writer, and anticipated the next question.

'—yes, I never told you, I suppose I thought you'd pick it up for yourself over there. You would have too, if you hadn't been too grand for Kilburn! Anyway the girl ran away after a few weeks; she came from Clanboffin so I suppose it was all you could expect – not that I believe all I hear about her.'

Eileen could only laugh at the number of targets her mother had pelleted.

'Come on, Mum, we've been over and over that Kilburn thing. Sure what was the point of going to England if I was only to be going to meet the same people I'd see here? And maybe Benny's wife was not all bad – why must it have been her fault?'

Mrs Tuohy did not reply as she put the shining delft on the table, but the nod of her head and the pursed mouth were enough to remind Eileen that if she had bothered with the Irish community in London she could have met a grand big builder and be living in Hampstead now like her sister instead of back here in Manortreacy as plain as when she left it and, so far as she could see, not half so Catholic.

'What I will say, Miss, is that nobody here has a bad word to say to Benny Cronin. He has a man and a boy working out there for him now and he's never seen with a drop too much or with a cigarette in his mouth. And his bull took a first prize in Leixlip last year!'

For a second her educated mind tempted Eileen to

question the significance of Benny's bull as part of this list of recommendations, but she sighed to herself as she prepared for a meeting later that evening, thinking 'poor Benny' before grabbing her folder of notes for the teachers she was to talk to. In the darkening street, with the sleet wind pushing winter into her bones as she walked, he came into her mind again and she smiled at the rueful thought of himself, and herself, after their different journeys, both back where they had started.

She wondered if his return had been a matter of choice, like hers. Did his marriage mean he had found romance, as she had – although, as she fervently and frequently thanked God, she had not felt the need to marry in order to keep hold of what she had found, and now she was free. Older, but free.

Now was all that true? Would she have married if she had been asked? Was there nobody whom she had wanted to marry? Impatient with herself and her habit of constant assessment, Eileen told herself that whether it was true or not now she'd had enough of it all anyway. Enough, as she scanned the marriages of the friends she'd left behind her, to last her lifetime. 'I'm finished with all that,' she told herself, and did not ask herself if it were true, and God did not strike her dead with a thunderbolt.

To give her her due she earnestly wanted to be free of emotional complexities. The odd thing was – and it was odd, she had admitted that much to herself long ago – that her studiously progressive professional life had been carried on against a sexual career that could only be described as chequered. She had not been promiscuous, but when she thought men loved her she was ready to love them back. Now it amounted to no more than a tedious passage of her life which concluded with her voluntary self-immurement in a small school in the Scottish highlands.

It was hardship I needed, she thought when she thought about it. And the shame of seeing people live easily in a land which seemed so bleak, providing for themselves without help from elsewhere; I needed to learn that one could live anywhere.

For years she had waited to see some grand design, some place for herself in a pattern. Instead she had come to understand that it is one's own pattern-making which makes the whole, and that the design of her life could be determined only by herself. That took courage, and besides, she was a slow learner. Trembling on a surging highland promontory she had remembered her grandmother's adage: experience is a hard school, but fools learn in no other.

She had learned enough to be able to respond to a newspaper advertisement for a position in the new library in Manortreacy sent without comment by her mother. She applied successfully and went home to an unsurprised town which had somehow carried on without her; few people understood why she had left Manortreacy, even fewer wondered why she came back to it.

As a librarian with teaching qualifications the service for schools was Eileen's special responsibility, and she did not spend much time in the public lending rooms. However, it was there that she met Benny Cronin, on a day of howling grimness when the building stank of damp warmth. He had brought back a Frederick Forsyth and an Anthony Trollope, he was taking out a Canon Sheehan and an Anthony Trollope, and her task was to tell him that his request for an inter-library loan of *Orley Farm* had not yet been filled.

'Eileen?' He was uncertain, but there was a tentative smile. 'Eileen! I'd heard you were back, but it's really good to see for myself – how are you?'

'Glad to be here. I think. I enjoy the work anyway. I gather things are going nicely for you too? You seem to have lots of time for reading, these days.'

Was it strange that there was no shyness between them? He confessed that he loved old-fashioned books now that he had to run a modern farm. As a child Eileen had accompanied her mother on visits to his mother, and anticipated some changes since then.

'Yes, there are changes, of course. But I let the stream alone, and I keep a few animals on a small scale, ducks and a few geese and hens.'

'And a gander?' That belligerent beak had terrified the small Eileen; Benny would be sent out to bring her safely past the bird.

They had never been particular friends, he was bigger and older and more solitary than she was as a child, and when school events or family visits had brought them together he had been kind to her, but no more. That left some liking between them, and now they were so much older, some curiosity.

With a patiently knowing line of customers lining up behind him, Benny suggested talking over their adventures. It was settled as a visit to Eileen's home, for tea with her mother.

'I suppose you arranged all that before the whole town,' was Mrs Tuohy's comment, but she had no real fear of Eileen being talked about, the girl was past the age for it.

When Benny came the winter had turned, and from his car he brought bunches of early daffodils for Mrs Tuohy which so disarmed her that she didn't see the small but elaborate box of chocolates he handed to Eileen in the hall. The evening went well: he ate enough to endear him to Eileen's mother, and to Eileen for her mother's sake. Although his talk was slow and deliberate he was not dull, and he and Eileen spelt out stories of their early, innocent London days. Mrs Tuohy talked about the people of the town, and together they remembered her husband, Eileen's father, and the children of the family now all spread throughout the country – indeed, the world.

'Except for Eileen,' Mrs Tuohy said once, and Benny turned to look at the brown-haired, brown-eyed young woman, graceful now where she had been neat, amused where she had been merry, and smiled his pleasure at her presence.

New because it was unexpected, this added ingredient

in Eileen's life of telephone calls, a film, a walk, gave a new dimension to the comforts of normality. It was nice after all, she thought, to be among real friends.

It was when her mother had seen the primroses, wrapped in damp moss and delivered in a box by the postman, that Mrs Tuohy had first called Benny the swain.

'My God, girl,' she said drily, 'what are you doing to that boy at all? He's like a swain, sending flowers to the house!'

Her face lightening as she read the little card over her breakfast coffee, Eileen said only that he knew she preferred flowers to sweets, that was all. It wasn't all. The card reminded her that she had once delighted in the primroses gleaming along the green banks of the stream below Benny's pastures. No more than that, though it was a notice that there was more to life than friendship.

She bought Wellington boots, took her car on hazardous mountain tracks, sweated as she helped with a difficult calving, not thinking much of what she was doing except that it was a kind of sharing. Perfume came in the post, a book found in Westport, a letter explaining an absence.

'A letter from your swain!' Eileen's mother called one morning, and on the hall table Eileen found the familiar writing stroked across the patch of envelope. It was the early, mellow beginning of a balmy day in April, and Eileen felt that lifting of the spirit which seemed to come these days when she thought of Benny. She held the envelope lightly, and the big black letters were a mirror through which she could see him, the dark brown hair crusted with grey, the long shape of him in his careless flannels or correct tweeds, the hazel eyes sober in his weathered face. His mouth, thinner now, was still as beautifully cut as she had noticed in adolescence, the nose as straight, the brows as sleek. She felt as she mused that he was looking at her, and she could not meet his eyes.

He had never touched her. She had had no expectation

of it, and it had never happened. Now she wondered. A fan of radiant flowers on the wall reflected the warming light in the window above the door, and in its glow she realized that she had never written to Benny, never given him anything. Here she felt, she suspected, that he was hoping for something.

Sitting down to her egg she opened the letter. He was taking a Jersey cow to Dublin, one of her pets. If she could get leave, would she like to accompany him?

Quickly, the answer was no. She decided she could not get the time off, but without asking, or taking time. To refuse nicely she searched the town for a card which might take the sting out of the message: the print was of a child in a field of corn, both child and grain blessed and golden with ripening sun. Again she stood with a message in her hands, unable again to think of looking at him.

Posting it, she said, 'I'm caught.' She would not go, but as she walked back along the street to the library, she knew she wanted to be with him. There was still something in herself which made her want to see what would happen. 'To be in his power', and she quivered as if to a remembered sting. Setting briskly to work she tried to keep her mind off the image of him, blocking it with the mounds of books before her, the accounting slips and invoices, the destination of each parcel. There was a request for *The Way We Live Now*, one of Benny's favourite Trollope novels. She turned over the pages, finding again the sad suit of Roger Carbury: 'After all, though love is a wonderful incident in a man's life, it is not only that he is here for.'

Duties. 'When did you realize you were stuck?' he had asked her as they walked, hands in anorak pockets, down a hill path.

'When I bought the car with my mother, so that we could "get around together". Then, I knew.' Lightly said.

For Benny it had been when he took on John Joe Sweeney.

'Not only did I have someone relying on me for wages, I gave him the bawn house. And when you give a man wages and a roof over his head, you're stuck. So I settled myself to it then.'

He had halted to light his pipe, and the tiny curl of flame lit up the slender black hairs of his eyebrows, the deep crease between his gathered eyes. The wet track was bedded with leaves, with twigs and mosses and bordering weeds. The cool of the spring evening had its own scent, but over that lay the velvet aroma of tobacco. This was what she scented as she counted and checked through the volumes. It was his smell that came, not the spicy earth or the chill. He had tossed aside the spent match and ground it into earth that was his own.

He was settled. Was she? How badly she wanted to think she was. After all, this was not new to her, this heightened sense of a being beyond her own. She knew what was happening. After all those mistakes it seemed that while she could hold to her resolution for herself she could not forbid it for others. She had made that error with Benny, the error of assumption.

'Everyone knows about my mistakes,' he had said, weeks ago only. They sat in a lounge bar and drank amiable pints of beer on their way home from the annual Head of the River race.

'You must admit, being the death of my father was a hard act to follow – but I followed it, and everyone knows all about it. What mistakes did you make? Is there a great secret?'

He was pretending a mystery of her own to show that he accepted her knowledge of him, but there was hurt in what he said although he said it almost gaily, making light of it. Sugar crystals sparkled on the dark, coffee-ringed table-top between them, a white brightness which linked itself in her mind with the hint of damage in his voice. She felt forced to honesty, beyond it, to the search for some truth in herself.

'I was lucky, Benny,' she said. 'Just lucky. I made

the silent kind of mistakes, the kind you recognize afterwards, but that seemed worth the risk at the time. All that happened was that I lost my taste for it, hadn't the courage any more, I suppose.'

'Was that why you went to Scotland?' His question was gentle, but it surprised her. He had been studying her. Only the instinct of understanding read through their casual conversations but she wasn't sure she wanted to be understood. Yet Benny deserved the truth if she could tell it.

She hesitated over it. 'More than that. I mean, yes, I was afraid I wouldn't want ever again to meet challenge. And I badly needed to feel that I could live with myself. By myself.'

'And can you?'

'Yes. Yes, Benny, I can.' She looked at him squarely then. He might as well know she was independent, looking for nothing. He might as well know everything.

'There is one mistake that wasn't so lucky. Just plain stupid, really. And I kept on making it.'

He was still, sitting easily back from the table, his hands in his pockets.

She went on quickly:

'I slept with men who didn't love me. I thought they did. I always thought they did.'

She thought the silence trembled between them. Then he said, 'But you didn't marry.'

Again she was surprised.

'Marry? No, of course not. I found out in time.'

'Well,' Benny said, the words serious but somehow light, 'that's the difference between us. You found out in time. I didn't.'

Kneeling between the books in the library, Eileen knew that he had absolved her. He was the only one in Manortreacy who knew about her life in England, and he had equated it with his own, saying they were different in the same way.

She had posted the rejecting card on her way to work. Going home later she wished she could recall it. Many

58

times in the days after that Eileen wished harder, wrenched with a kind of hopeless regret. Then when it was time for Benny to be back from Dublin and days after that time again, a kind of fright took hold of her. When the telephone rang in her office she jumped and steadied herself before answering. It was never him. Her mother noticed.

'I hear your swain won all round him in Dublin.' She was reading the *Chronicle* by the light of the window, but pretended her information came through more natural, subtle channels.

'Is he coming in to town at the weekend?'

There was a black slug of jam at the edge of Eileen's plate; the blackcurrants had cropped heavily and the kitchen was still full of the bright warm smell of their cooking. The house was comfortable, a well-used, well-kept building, characteristic of the town in its main-street elegance. At this time of evening the summer light was deepening to gold, and the geraniums in their old china pots were stippled as if with sequins. Getting up heavily and rinsing the dishes before washing them in the sink, Eileen wondered if this would be enough for her for the rest of her life. She had chosen it; would it be enough?

'I don't know what Benny plans to do this weekend,' she said to her mother, casually as if to give the impression that he and she together had talked about it. Mrs Tuohy wasn't fooled for a moment, saying only that she had a lot of gardening and preserving to do so wouldn't want to be taken anywhere in the car if Eileen was wondering. Her daughter was free, in other words, to make plans.

Freedom was a very relative thing, Eileen reflected as she went for a searching, restless walk in that most poignant time of a summer evening, when soft purple rain soaks perfume from the lime trees and the white globes of philadelphus hang heavy and sweet. From the boat club came submerged music from the Friday night dance, and the alleys and angles of the town smoked with blue dusk. She returned soused in self-pity, but there was the beginning of shame underneath it, an awareness of selfishness.

Without Benny, and missing him dreadfully because she was uncertain, she had begun to count. The letters, the cards, the bunched or potted flowers, the walks and the drives, all had come from him. That could be said to be in the nature of things, perhaps, but somehow to remember it now made her uncomfortable. Bigger than that, however, was the patience of his attentions. There was a generosity in him and she had accepted it. Beyond all that there was Benny himself, the person that he was, not so much his value although she valued him, but his essence.

That had been offered too. And what had she thought she preferred? Her own calm stoicism. That, instead of the sense of him in her blood, the way her pulse thumped at this incisive thought of him as a man as she had known men, lusty and endearing but different because he was Benny.

'In the morning,' she promised herself, 'I'll take the car and go up to him. I can do that much. I'll go to him and see what happens.'

It was almost exciting, going to bed with that thought. The optimism of her resolution kept her awake with dreams of what would happen, but the cheerful dawn found her at last chill, no longer sure, dreaming all done. Six o'clock was too early, even for a farmer. As the hours grew she felt her purpose draining. By eight she still could have gone, by nine the thought of her mother's questions held her back, by ten it was the fear of making a fool of herself.

What right, after all, did she have to be asking for explanations? The man was his own boss, they were both adults, he had only stayed away from her for a few days. Ten and a half days. At his age he wouldn't like to have to answer for himself in that way.

At her age, too. 'Thirty-six,' she said to herself, 'that's not the age to be taking risks. It would be better to leave it, we'll meet around the town and it'll be all right.'

Except that she'd never find out what had happened. Never atone. There was that side to being an adult, too. The duties of maturity. Attempting to put right was one of them, wasn't it? Reparation took courage – and she had thought she had that. It was strange too, disquieting, to feel the need for courage with Benny. Now there were all sorts of needs stampeding at her, needs she had recognized and banished and which now came clambering back into her consciousness and above them all, clamouring most insistently, was the need for Benny himself. It was a risk, it would be a risk, he might not want her, but she was ready to give anything he wanted.

What could she bring him? The white geraniums grown from seed on the sitting-room window. Pots of the currant jam glazing the pantry shelves, a blue-leaved bunch of the striped and dappled pinks all spiced and giddy-smelling, that paperback of Cobbett's *English Gardener* she'd discovered. And wine, the bottle bought in case he came to dinner and never opened. A good year, she hoped.

Brushed and bare-legged in a skirt of improbably flowered cotton and chaste white shirt, feeling brave and wretched at the same time, she drove too soon over the six miles to the farm. Getting out to lift the latch of the first gate she felt her hands damp against the wrought iron.

'I know what I'm doing,' she told herself sharply against her clenched eyes, and she went on over the cattle grid and up the drive until the house stood square and uncompromising before her.

Benny had seen her coming, and pounded up from the small barn, his ecstatic collie dancing under his feet, nearly tripping him. He slowed before he reached her so that she would not see him red and sweating with haste. She stood by the car, her arms like a belt between the flowers of her skirt and the heaving blossoms she

61

held. Above them her face shone, she couldn't help it, she was so glad to see him.

'Oh, I am so *glad* to see you, Benny!' she cried, and he laughed out loud at the joy in her voice, and reached out to grasp her. He could have congratulated himself that at last she had come to him but instead he held on to her so that book and flowers and parcels rolled and tumbled onto the gravel as the upright bodies met. Spirit and flesh blazed between them like the morning's second sun; their rapture was filtered through the green of the bounding fields, through the brick-red barns and the true and limpid river winding below the hill of the farmhouse to the grey distance of the town.

'By God, girl,' was all Benny could say. 'By God!' His voice was unsteady against her hair. 'I thought I'd gone the wrong way about it . . .'

'I thought I'd never make it past the gander!' She was able to laugh at last, although still frightened, frightened now that she had nearly not made it.

Benny had to remind her that there would be other ganders to pass. The Canon. Her Mother.

'Ah, Benny, we'll make it now. As for my mother, she knows that every blessing is a mixed one, and she doesn't much care what the mix is any more!'

They did Mrs Tuohy an injustice. She would have no trouble at all in accepting Benny as a son-in-law. She knew Eileen, and knew how dangerously her daughter had been living. And besides, she had always had a soft spot for the swain.

Internal Assonance

Love is a matter of coincidence: the wrong man in the right place. We are not supposed to want love stories, and this is not one of them, for I have never asked myself what happened or what it meant although I am sure that he knew and I knew that something had happened. If I tried to pretend, to build anything on it, it would only come to this: that he was drunk and I was not. If I remember I must remember that, too. Nor is it even always a matter of memory, but of consciousness: when driving alone at night along a quay-side street I feel gulls rise through the lamplight and fall like a flock of stars. I turn to exclaim to the person who is with me in my mind and it is him.

I wanted to put a shape on this story, to use memory like a moulded bowl. Then I saw that shape is another word for perspective, and that all I was doing was looking from a distance, and backward.

It was summer, a time of festivals, and the city glowed with geraniums and self-congratulation, it hummed to a confident rhythm. This happens still, and one year never reminds me of another, or of the one in which he occurred. There is nothing left of that, he need never have passed through.

The fact that he did, that Mark Dormann appeared in town, was a resounding coup for the ageing organizers of this one year, this one event. He turned up in a manageable condition too, in itself a great relief to the reception committee: year after year its members could be seen grappling with the social consequences of notorious eccentricities, well-publicized diversions which comprehensively eclipsed their own ebullient coarsenesses. Few of these had ever read a word in verse or prose written by Mark Dormann or, to judge from their conversation, by anyone else either.

There was no need to apologize for that. Their function was to get famous names into the city for one week of the year, justifying an extension of pub opening hours and claiming a little notice from complacent university lecturers to warm their own existence. For them it was enough that his name had a loud glamour; his presence rather than his work excited interest, his name peppered savoury column inches in the English dailies. That was enough.

'Mark Dormann?' The features editor was puzzled. 'Isn't he a bit over-written these days? What's new about him?'

'The fact that he's here!' I had no right to be indignant, I wasn't sure what I wanted to do about it myself.

'You think he might be on the way down, on the slide?'

He was looking at that morning's crop of pictures. Dormann with a local poet so full of beer that his face might have been painted with Vaseline; they were both pouring champagne over a blonde girl who looked, to give her her due, as if she was hating it. Suddenly the pictures hurt me.

'There's more to him than this. I'm sure there is. He didn't write "Promenade" out of that kind of vacancy; perhaps an interview now would get him to say just what's going on. And anyway he's too big to ignore completely . . .'

The editor wasn't sure that anyone would be interested. There was something unflattering to us both that we should be surprised at Mark Dormann's appearance in our city, yet that surprise in itself provided an excuse for a story, especially as I had long before won the right to avoid events such as the Festival altogether and therefore on this occasion would be bringing a less familiar, more questioning attitude to examining it. Like the editor I didn't think anyone who mattered would be interested otherwise.

Also, like most sources of contemporary fame, those of Mark Dormann were hard to define; even in retrospect they are still. Certainly prolific without ever relinquishing a recognized standard, he had produced notable publishing successes and later more splendid screen achievements. Very handsome in a worn style, he had been a partner in a sumptuous marriage which linked him to minor English nobility and major American wealth. A woman of renowned beauty and talent, his wife had died a lonely death which, given who she was, could not be private, the only obvious privilege loneliness confers.

Not knowing him or ever expecting to at that time I remember how the tributes hinted, in several cases, that he had not been the only one to love her or know her intimately, that his grief was not unique. If that was betrayal, at least she had nothing to do with it.

So if you couldn't say that his life-style was notorious, it was public. Without quite thinking about it at that time, I sensed within myself some trace of kinship; in a city addicted to gossip, I was leading a life which could only survive by no one knowing anything about it. That emerged as a kind of sympathy, making it easier for me to consider my approach to Mark Dormann as one being made in the name of truth, rather than of journalistic impertinence. At that time I was not yet aware that the conscious effort to be a good journalist in ethical as well as career terms induces a sense of superiority which is as false as anything a 'bad' journalist can do. And I was young, and still believed in curiosity as sufficient motivation.

But things happen to us. Changing handbags is a big event in my domestic life, and I avoid it for years. That very week however I had abandoned my satchel for the sake of summer style and had rescued from the obscurity of the top shelf of the wardrobe an altogether neater purse.

When I saw the letters, three of them, for a minute I did not recognize the handwriting. Then I remembered. That bag and their disposal within it had been part of the act described by Emily Dickinson as 'The sweeping up of the heart/and putting love away'. It must have worked. I had forgotten that I had them. Being reminded like this was not comfortable. Confidence fled before these hints of pain, I did not want it, I did not open the letters. I put them on the dressing table among the ornamental trinkets, at a corner where I could see them from the corner, indeed, of my eye. That was enough, then.

From that corner they cast no shadow on my life. When I drove to the landscaped hotel gloating above summer lawns there were flowers in my straw hat, the sun filtered through the hairs of my bare arms, there was an expansive ease in all the widest parts of my mind; my research was done and adequate for 800 words even if this famous author, really just another famous author, was asleep or drunk or incapable or unbearably rude – all possibilities any journalist learns to expect.

He was only drunk. The understanding smile of the receptionist hinted at something. 'He's in his room,' she said. 'You can go up, you're expected. Give me a ring if you want anything . . .'

The room was full of light, the pale furnishings suggesting an insubstantial opulence in which the most positive shape was his own where he sat in a curtained shadow. Without standing he welcomed me efficiently, even with some warmth; he was glad of company, although it soon became obvious that he had an agonizing hangover. He gestured me to a window-seat, and from this perch I heard the voices of children in the garden. He told me, slowly, their ages, all under twelve; he spoke as if he was reassuring himself that to keep them with him was the best thing to do.

'For them, or for you?' I asked my questions sharply. My job was to make this man reveal himself. I settled to my assertive questioning: the genealogy of *Shadow to Shadow*, for example, had led critics to expect continuing attention to the Industrial Revolution. Yet his next book, *Wyatt*, had been a biography which, not at all afraid of upsetting him as my voice declared itself, I called 'romantic'. I was taking a crisp, intelligent line about the books. We would get on to the poetry later, to the films later still. Now in charge, I was more amused by this situation than dismayed by it, and I was on the way to a nice little interview piece.

What had brought him from Kipling to Thomas Wyatt?

He brought his eyes around to focus on me. I sat against the light, and the light hurt him. He winced in a slow spasm and I saw, in the turning of his face, the grey skin beneath the tan, the colours of weariness, not just discomfort, tainting the whole look of him.

'You know Wyatt, do you?'

From his book, I knew some of the poetry. 'They flee from me that sometime did me seek/With naked foot . . .' was all I could offer, making a question of it. Then I remembered: there had been more, that grade A for Eng. Lit. at school had been deserved:

'Forget not yet the tried intent
Of such a truth as I have meant,
My great travail so gladly spent,
Forget not yet.'

There was no embarrassment in this. I was showing off. But then his voice came in, measuring the calm cadences:

'Forget not yet, forget not this,
How long ago hath been and is
The mind that never meant amiss.
Forget not yet.'

So, there the three of us were, the author, myself and Wyatt, caught by the chip of chance. My notebook lay in my lap. The children's voices still sounded from

67

outside, not distant, but not of immediate concern.

'You told me your name,' he said, asking for it again. He repeated it after me, and I blushed at the thought that he might want to remember it, to remember me. He asked who I wrote for, what I wrote, all questions to locate what I was doing here in this room with him in this city. I realized then, only slowly because the tempo of this meeting had changed and our exchange was imposing its own rhythm, that he had begun by putting up with me because he had been asked to. His grasp on what happened to him was loosening so that he could no longer hold on to smaller events, things had to be large and self-evident for him to be able to control them.

'Anne,' he said after a silence in which we tried to accommodate each other, 'Anne, if you were going to commit suicide by cutting your wrists, what book would you choose to read while waiting for the blood to flow out?'

'*Cranford.*' I immediately accepted the preposterous notion, understanding at once that this was precisely what would make that form of death bearable to me.

To his 'why', I said that Mrs Gaskell talks so directly to the reader, taking you into her confidence, one would feel that one had company.

'You couldn't do it alone, then?'

No, I said. I couldn't do that entirely alone. As I spoke I saw his eyes grow distant again and felt the shock of wondering if that was what she had done, how she had died.

He must have seen the flush of my dismay.

'Do you mind if I have a drink? Would you like something, or is it too early? Coffee, perhaps?'

He made the social offering without moving. It was I who phoned room service, ordering his gin and my coffee as a way of covering a new awkwardness. He smiled when he heard me ask for coffee – 'You're going to stay in charge, are you?' I smiled too; I was.

'Look,' he said, drawing me back to the window as we

68

waited. 'That's our governess. She takes good care of the children, very good care . . .' We agreed that this was important, children needed continuity. The gin arrived and he drank with energy. The woman's voice had joined the others outside and the small sounds faded together as they moved away through the trees. We could start again and I drank hot coffee to get my mind back on the proper track. I could ask him about his life, the effect of critical success, the time in America, even deep questions of personal philosophy. But now I did not want to.

His voice had begun to slip once more, its yeasty distinction blurring as his face was blurred, the contours softening. The silence between us deepened into a languor and the air was heavy with a new awareness of one another. My smart competence died into the warmth we did not want to disturb.

By the time he spoke to me again, I had remembered the letters, silent on my dressing table. When the sun shone through the window I could see each white rectangle reflected in the mirror with the pot-pourri, the scent-bottles, the silver cream spoon, the glass animals from Italy, the swathed beads. I could open them now, I thought now that I felt my being had a dimension which could contain the things that happen without crippling me.

'Do something for me, Anne.' His voice startled me, although he spoke softly.

'Lie down with me on that divan over there; I'll tell you the story of my life. Will you do that?'

I could not take my eyes from his as I sought the meaning of his words, but I felt the bed behind me almost as if it were growing from the wall, dappled with sun and with flowers, inviting.

My hesitation was not from surprise, but from a desire not to hurt him. I like to think now that I refused with some grace. All he wanted was comfort, I think, yet he lived at a distance from me, and weak sex was not the way to bridge that gap. But I did not want him to think badly of me. I must have known, I suppose, that he had become part of the story of my life.

Accepting the refusal, he held my hand, his dark head thrown back against the leather of the armchair so that his stretched throat looked taut and vulnerable. He closed his eyes when he spoke:

'Are you a Catholic? You believe in guilt, don't you, that it's wrong to despair?'

A Catholic? In the once upon a time sense, yes; and it was true that from all that I had learned I believed that final despair was a sin, although an understandable one.

He asked me about suicide, again. That was where despair came into it, of course, but it had been a late development for him. His early work, especially his poetry, had been lambent with optimism; even misplaced optimism was either funny or tragic, not hopeless. I told him I had thought that as a writer he had not fallen for the soft, indulgent lures of self-pity. Daring through this soft intimacy, I said that I thought suicide was a particularly mean form of revenge, used by people who had lost their grip on life but preferred to blame others for the loss. And those others could never explain, or make any reparation.

He wanted more gin. I poured it for him. It was time for me to go, but I could not leave him like this, lonely and doubting. I told him about the rat. My rat.

Where I live there is a garden and a cat, and a tree in the garden in which the cat loves to sit. One day in the spring before that summer I sighed when I heard frenzied squeaking, thinking I would have to set about the messy and usually useless business of rescuing a bird, but it was not a bird. It was a rat, and the cat had treed him. He clung, swaying, to a long dipping branch, a branch laden with the fruit of his weight, too slight to hold the cat which crouched on the ground instead, tense, alert, limitlessly patient. I ran for the sweeping brush and began to beat it against the branch, praying Oh God don't let him fall on me, Oh God, let Tarka catch him.

And then the sun came out. In the amiable light the

cat shone black and orange and white against the speckled grass. A few translucent roses hung beneath the wisteria, whose purple bunches spiced the ardent air with sweetness.

To the top of the topmost branch of the pear tree the rat clung, the froth of blossom all around him, his claws like talons piercing the grey bark. The sun had caught him but he held on, silent, desperately clutching. His features shone out clear. The coat was glossy grey and brown, the ears pressed back in his near-panic to the small skull, the snout, wet and wide-nostrilled, had each glistening whisker separate and distinct. He was a burnished animal, and I could see the tender pink skin between the claws of his toes as they gripped the scaley branch. I felt his despair, I felt his courage.

The cat did not know what had happened as I scooped her into my arms and held her firmly so she could not escape. I let the brush fall gently to the ground and we withdrew from the rat's arena. The quality of his courage had defeated my fear of him, and I could not even look from a window to see what happened in case, on retreating backward down the tree at last he might look ridiculous, or cunning, or somehow belittled. But he had not belittled himself by taking the last way out, by falling.

It was a small story to tell, and I was telling it for the first time, not quite understanding what I wanted to say. In the silence which followed I made the officious gestures of departure, the notebook, the hat and hand-bag, the extended hand. Suddenly the room was small, he had got out of the armchair and stood hugely in front of me, holding the glass steadily in his hand.

'And wilt thou leave me thus?
Say nay, say nay, for shame,
To save me from the blame
Of all my grief . . .'

It was Prospero I thought of, the room had become a magic isle; there is still a scent of magic about the

71

memory. I found myself liking him intensely. He dwarfed his surroundings, there was a nobility to him, he deserved to be taken seriously. He had the gift of transformation, perhaps not of himself, but of those around him.

I smiled at him, and put my hand up to touch his face, and he smiled and touched me behind my left ear and along the shadow of my jaw. He let me go.

In the corridor three black-headed children came scampering along, behind them like a shepherd a slender young woman who had no expression at all on her face as she looked at me.

At the office the next morning there was a message to ring the hotel. His charming, fermented voice made a graceful and complete apology. If I would care to meet him again he would of course tell me anything I wanted to know. We met over coffee in the smart little lounge and he was the obliging sober and successful author. We had a very intelligent and good-humoured and even funny little interview as though we had never met before or at least had only met at a party. When it was over and I was about to go he asked courteously if I had all I wanted. He added – 'Perhaps you were too sensitive: you never asked about my wife. We did not speak of her yesterday.'

I thought we had talked of nothing and no one else, but could not say that.

'No, we did not speak of her. Or indeed, about my poetry. I don't write much now, you know, not much poetry. But I was a poet, once, I think I still am. I wrote poetry while I lived with her, she gave my life its sound. She was my internal assonance . . .'

It took me a few days to write the article. First, I opened the letters. The editor said it was a good piece, but with one great mistake. It suggested hidden knowledge, the last thing a journalist may indicate without divulging it. So, it was not the interview of my career, perhaps, but it was not an important failure.

There were other failures, and I suffered, but I had

been right to open the letters, to have the courage for that at least, for hope.

He married the governess, and finished his last book. He died from natural causes, and not alone. A friend rang to tell me. 'I know you cared for him,' she said, her voice worried along the wire. But I had no right to care, really, had I? It was only that something had happened, and that I recognized the source of his last title, *The Long Perspectives*. It was from Philip Larkin: 'The long perspectives that link us to our losses . . .'

Epiphany

It is an unlikely place for a tree, so near the beach. Sometimes a rambling cow from the fields across the road used it as a scratching post, but this is not what has bent it into its leaning, straining shape. It is not the leisurely strength of the bodies of animals which has spread its branches inward towards the land, so that its few summer leaves scatter in autumn not on to the reeking shore beneath, but down on the friendlier path leading to the road and to the meadows beyond the dunes.

The tree has its winter shape from the wind. In winter the pressure of fierce air tugs and tugs its branches further from the sea, away from that horizon, gleaming even in the cold, where the sunlight while it lasts holds a liquid brightness in a line between the water and the sky.

Although it is turned in towards the townlands and the homesteads, the tree is enchanted by the sea which pulls at its back, by the tide, by the surge which in the deadness of the year throws salty spray against its bark, which teases and trickles around it while all the other spilt and angry water runs slowly back in channels through the dunes.

Bent and bitter though it may look, the tree on its dune is so solitary, so strange, that it gathers the landscape in towards itself, as if it were a target on which all the sights are narrowed. From the sea its posture is a curve, a slow and helpless leaning, an attitude of obeisance and humility. From this curving everything around it slides out and along and inevitably down into the waiting tide.

The spread of fields behind the dunes is hidden, but from the highest point of the sandy hillock on which the tree is perched the fringed meadows, the weedy and slothful river, the indifferent pebbled sands, the crumbling caved rocks rambling further away to where the dunes lift into cliffs, all these stretch and glide their way lazily to the sea, wherever it chooses to halt its restless lunge inland.

In summer the tidemark fluctuates, its dips and surges marked by seaweed and wrack. Now the tree is at its best, leaved for a while, a sour green shade on the grass beneath the branches. Many times, but long ago, when the sisters were children of different ages, this was *the* beach, accessible by bus and even by bicycle, the point of many happy journeys of summertime. Now that three of these four sisters have reached the unimaginable years of forty, now that their married lives have come to be lived close to one another, close to home as they put it themselves, for their children too this is the beach, the point of this day's journey.

At this time, and at this age, the older sisters see themselves as a group to which the youngest has only recently, on her marriage, been admitted. Their consciousness of the years they have spent alive has merged into a general belief that though they are no longer officially young, not even what they themselves might anxiously term young, they are, at least, 'young enough'. After absences no longer than two weeks of holidays, they exclaim over one another with pleasure and gratification, measuring more acutely than they assess their various children. Those after all are the children, who will be young in that future which contains nothing for the mothers except ageing and then age. Their pleasure in one another has some element of corporate sustenance. 'How well you're looking,' they say, meaning, 'How well you're holding out, how well we're all holding out.'

There is nothing crude about this; they have all learned discretion. They chide whichever one of them applies the new bronze rouges too enthusiastically, but they also dislike the fact that one of them disputes the need to use it at all. And sometimes three of them together consider the fourth, the youngest, cigarette on her lip and first child on her hip, the gloss on her skin all her own – they have asked – the bounce of her hair and of her walk and the self-confidence of her smile shining at them, their secret security. They look at her and listen to her and later suggest to one another that it is time for another effort to get Patsy to stop smoking. Whatever about her lungs, her teeth will be ruined.

Now in this summer, under this tree, the thin plume of smoke from Patsy's cigarette moves briefly against the air. The sisters are preparing a picnic; the bus that used to bring them almost here – there was quite a way to walk – has been discontinued, and they have driven, as usual, in the two cars owned by the sisters who are members of two-car families. Because they started late, and Maura got lost – 'Maura would get lost going to Mass!' muttered Helen, waiting at the signpost – the beach was quiet when they all arrived, but it is still hot summer here, where the air is trapped between the dunes and the curve of the shore.

The sun through the leaves of the tree dapples the cloth which Helen has spread on the spiky grass. The four corners are held down against the breeze with stones cheerfully supplied by the children, this part of the ritual being essential to their comfort by now. The food has not yet been unpacked, it is too soon, and too warm, but the bottles of ginger beer and lemonade and orange juice are hidden, with the large bottle of light Italian wine, under layers of jackets and jumpers which, brought in order to keep the children warm on the way home, are now being used to keep the drinks cool, hiding them from the sun.

This rattling pile is laid against the stem of the tree, too thin for a trunk as it leans away from the water, and

76

here also the dog beloved of Helen's children has flopped down, eager for some little shade before he tears off down the beach again, in answer to the fluting whistle of one of the boys.

Scattered along the sand, among the rocks, at the edges of the tide, the children look as if they have been tossed carelessly high away from the dunes, to land anywhere the cast might fling them, thrown like bright pebbles into the aura of the day. From this distance they glisten, moving in an indolent but particular pattern of their own. There are nine of them. Round and brown and gentle, Patsy's little boy sits at the edge of a very small pool, his ankles lost in its water and soft weeds. He is the kind of child, Patsy often thinks, who not only puts up his face for your kiss, but smiles as he does so, a tender acceptance of love. Around him are scattered the tools of whatever trade he may decide on: bucket and spade, goggles, a sunhat of piratical slant, a homemade fishing rod, a flag of red-flowered cotton on a bamboo stick, a gun.

The older boys play aggressive football in the slender waves, their tackles invigorated by showers of spray beaten from the water by the splash of their bodies. Two girls are swimming, one of them only a wet black head surging above the water, the other preferring to jump over each wave until the water reaches her hips, and then calls to her companion who turns back and laughs and dives towards her and together they jump back in again, hand in hand, towards the beach.

The rocks which cradle Patsy's child hide two more children, a boy and a girl, of different families but the same age; these two are natural allies in any squabble or question of demarcation. Now they are searching for shells or stones, sea-wrack small and brilliant enough to dazzle classmates when they return to school. They are at ease, secure in their own sense of time which has mapped out this afternoon for them.

Another child, the younger of Helen's two daughters, is struggling gallantly up the beach towards the small

77

boy and his pool. For her the beach is large and even lonely, the signposts on it are her mother on the dune beneath the tree, and her little cousin whose intent and mysterious games never exclude her. Safe now because she is watched over by one and making her way to the other, the child acknowledges the sun on her ripening skin, she sees and notes the gleam of light on the brown and rosy rocks, the glitter of water which will be warm when she puts her feet into the pool.

All the children, in jeans, swimming-togs, shorts and T-shirts, love this beach which even on crowded early days has room for them. They enjoy each other's company, luxuriate in the summer freedoms which this day, this sea and sand, this hot light, space filled with shining air, this gay and sunny seaside afternoon, this dog rollicking down to their whistle in plumes of hair and sand, this conjunction of mothers, will for ever represent to them, unless they forget it altogether.

Greta's eyes have been staring down at the far-flung children, identifying her own without anxiety. Now her lids feel rough, her eyes are smarting from the glare, from looking too long at the brightness around the three dark heads to which her life is leased.

'This is what fathers always miss,' she thinks, lying back against a beachbag, her arm bent up against her forehead. She smiles as she remembers Joe's last outing with them, herself and the children, that was only last weekend. Although he had been obediently eager at first, and nowhere had seemed to be too far to drive (she had kept him, with the wisdom of the experience of other summers, to resorts close to home) once on the beach he had begun to display the symptoms of acute physical discomfort, eventually leaving them in order to read the Sunday papers in some comfort in the car. He was almost shamefaced about this, and seemed to want to be able to share the children's enthusiasm, but other things became too much for him always, the heat, the sand in his sausage-roll, other people, his belly curving out over the waist-band of his swimming trunks. Still, it was his ritual obeisance to holidays, and Greta preferred to let everyone suffer a little for that one day than to exclude him altogether for the sake of comfort.

'But this is what he misses,' she thinks still, measuring the brown and healthy limbs flashing through the gentle surf. 'This is the feeling of their bodies, watching them grow, like flowers in a Walt Disney nature film, unfolding to the sun.'

Perhaps men wouldn't notice that kind of thing. Perhaps Joe didn't, although against that possibility had to be laid the undoubted fact that Joe certainly enjoyed seeing her limbs unfolding. They had met and married long after either of them had expected to do anything of the sort. Now when Greta remembers the amazement with which they encountered one another she wonders why she had ever let herself even think in phrases which allowed such words as 'falling in love' to be commonplace.

'I can only think of it in inverted commas,' she muses, rolling over on to her stomach in order to think of it in a more satisfactory way. She recalls how Joe, so burly and stoical, had admitted being shaken by his discovery of mature passion. They shook together, swept by the gales of their late thirties. It had all happened very fast. The decision was taken, although she had tried to talk calmly to herself, about not letting time become the deciding factor, the sense of this being their last chance. They took it, 'It was a chance,' Greta says to herself now. 'Chance, a risk. An adventure. What a chance to take. And only when we took it, and saw the extent of the risk we had each taken, it was only then that we began to fall in love.'

The other risk was the one which her sisters discussed earnestly with one another but very gently with her – the other decision, to have some children as quickly as possible. Given a starting age of thirty-eight, she and Joe had compromised at three, and achieved each conception, pregnancy, delivery and comprehensible male child, feeling themselves very lucky indeed. 'Oh, we have been so lucky,' Greta thinks every time she sees the stretch marks on her flaccid stomach, the wrinkles on her small breasts. It had turned out to be so easy, and in the relief of success and safety it had been easy also to agree that three was enough, there should be no more risks, and the last pregnancy had been the last child.

'Tied?' Helen asked, worried about mortal sin. But Maura and Patsy had been unequivocal in their approval, Maura especially having spent months worrying about how to suggest such a solution to Greta. Her rapturous response betrayed her relief and had startled Greta into feeling much older, much more threatened by her age, than ever since she had married.

'I'm still only forty-six,' she whispers to herself as she turns over to count her three tenants, the sun warm on the Clairol bronze of her hair.

'Mammy! Look!' a child's cry reaches her, and she lifts her hand from her hot forehead to acknowledge the claim for applause. Her waving fingers seem to catch the cry and turn it back to her: she hears her own voice calling long ago the same words along the same beach, and she sees her own mother reaching with long white legs across those rocks which shield the children now. Her mother's legs had sometimes had large mottled bruises near the thighs, stigmata which had fascinated her daughters. Greta plays over again in the space between her hand and her eyes the scene of her mother's legs stretching from the dune to the rocks to come to her, striated with blue flex, patched behind the knees, behind the instep, with those rosy-purple flares, varicose.

Sometimes Greta is still shocked at Mass that her mother isn't one of those women moving away from the altar-rails. 'I still can't believe she isn't there,' she thinks now, remembering the rose in the coffin. She still thinks sometimes that the tall woman turning back from the hand of the priest is her mother. How strange it seems that without her all the girls should be here, all so well, so many children of their own. 'She would be so pleased, to be with us.'

A phrase, a lament, comes in to her head. It is, she places it, from the book in her bag. Karen Blixen's grieving question – 'Does Africa know a song of me? Would the air over the plain quiver with a colour that I had on, would the children invent a game where my name was . . .?'

'Oh, Mammy,' cries Greta now, in the dark shadow of her hand against the sun. 'Oh Mammy, all our children know of you are photographs, a grave. But their lullabies are songs of you, we sing them to sleep with melodies we remember hearing first in your own voice. And sometimes, out walking, or playing cards, or baking in the kitchen, we tell stories where your name is. All my colours are colours from you, and it is true, our own motherhood has brought us back to you, although we have only become mothers since you died.'

Her mother died at fifty. Greta is not much younger. She has lately begun to identify both their lives, as though her loss can only be assuaged by absorption. Where her father is in this she hates to think. It's like being jealous; the realities of his marriage must have given him memories different to her own, although surely she and her sisters belong there too, but he must have a satisfaction, a recollection not just of happiness but of sometimes having been right, the more honest or the more honourable of the two. Knowing all this she resents the completeness of the life he has built up since that one death in the family, what in her irritation she calls his after-life.

'I'm not fair to him,' she reminds herself. 'I want him to be more lonely. But there's only one kind of loneliness that matters, and he has that. Why should I want more; after twenty years why do I still look for the change that it made, why do I still want the world to say – "we notice, we notice"? As though the world itself should have stopped?'

Wondering, she sits up to gaze again at the children vanishing and reappearing on the edges of the tide, busy between the shoulders of rock and crevice. Her feet dig for comfort into the sand that lies in drifts among the little tufts of grass, the sand that moves softly along her skin and then dribbles away between her toes.

Helen has begun to divide the bread into piles of buttered slices, which will come together again around lettuce, salami, circles of pale pink meat beloved of the children. The tomatoes and hard-boiled eggs she leaves in their plastic boxes, but the shakers of salt and pepper she puts in the middle of the cloth, hiding at the same time the little jar of salad-dressing Maura has brought as part of her supplies. She is relieved that this time Patsy has remembered to bake the apple tart in a rectangular tin rather than a pie-dish, and has even cut it into small squares for easier distribution.

There should be, Helen thinks, enough for everyone, although her eye has already decided on the number of sausage-rolls she is going to put aside for herself and the girls, her sisters, as insurance against the ravenous appetites now being built up on the beach, and against their shared maternal compulsion to feed the children first and probably best.

'We'll have to get over that, someday,' she says to herself firmly, and tucks Maura's salmon quiche neatly back into its napkin. 'It doesn't matter if it's only tinned, we love it, and they won't appreciate it and just this once we'll keep it to ourselves.' She tots up the times the children have poked at spinach and baked custards and pizzas she has offered at years of meals. Usually, she realizes, when her own father comes to lunch; she loves to offer food which he will know has been cooked especially for him. His mild protests and genuine pleasure console her for his life.

Spreading the plastic plates across the cloth, stirred by little tilts of breeze, her hands wander among the sandwiches, piling them and covering them with tea-towels so that their mysterious humps will appear even more enticing to the children. She is sorry that her father isn't with them. Perhaps he would have come if Kevin had agreed, but Kevin never came on these out-ings, none of the husbands came, each separate family had its own outings, each father, with varying regu-larity, joined them.

'Men are all the same, really,' Helen thinks. 'The truth is that neither Dad nor Kevin really enjoy picnics, they only come when they do because they might want a swim, or feel guilty because it's been so long since they were out with the children.'

What she doesn't say to herself, she doesn't feel com-fortable with this fact, is that she doesn't really miss the men. Her acceptance of their absence is always couched in terms of regret, but her sisters all know that like them but less obviously, she accepts that these few scattered days are better without husbands and fathers. It is what gives them their special charac-ter. Their own father was, of course, part of those early beach days, the 'long ago' days, but even then they seemed to sense an abstraction, as if his presence had been an effort of will, a decision, whereas they and their mother seemed to be answering some irresistible lure, pulled by a string even time had not broken.

'Anyway, if Kevin is happier not to come with us, that's the best for him. Although I'd be glad if he preferred coming. He should like being with us, a father should want to be with his wife and his children. Perhaps I take them out too often, though?' Ah, now this is a comforting possibility, perhaps his negligence is really all *her* fault, perhaps she doesn't have to criticize him at all.

'Besides, he's away today, he won't be home at tea-time, he won't be wanting a meal. I'll have a nice little supper ready for him when he gets in.' Helen discerns the shape of the quiche in its napkin. That, heated up, would be ideal. Perfect. And then, if she keeps enough

83

of it she can drop down to her father tomorrow and tell
him to heat it through for his own tea. He'll like that.
She'll bring the children and they might cut the grass
for him, and then they could watch his colour television. That's tomorrow, the grass, and Grandfather all
fixed up.

'Of course all this is going on round Maura's pie!'
Helen reminds herself with a laugh. As she leans over
to push the napkin more securely over the pastry she
feels again the pull of that knob under her arm. It's
three months now since she spoke to the doctor about
it, explaining how it got harder, more tender, just
before her period. He had said simply that yes, lots of
women had that little problem. Glands.

'This is ridiculous,' she tells herself, pushing away
the swelling urge to press her palms gently around her
breasts. She can do that at home, when she gets home
she can have a bath and then Kevin will be there and if
she's worried she'll talk to him about it. Well, no, perhaps it would be better not to say anything to Kevin.
It's too silly, making a fuss about nothing, and he'd
only be worried. And she is certainly not going to say
anything to the girls. No, she will examine herself at
home the way she saw in *Woman's Own*: she had kept
the diagrams, and as well there is the leaflet from the
Family Planning Clinic. 'It doesn't have to be cancer.
And then it doesn't have to be malignant. And look
how long Mammy lasted, how well she was, sometimes.'

She sits still. The weather around her is coloured with
white and smells of flowers, sluiced diarrhoea, disin-
fectant, a weight of warmth into which her mother's
words had crept in whispers from the hospital bed: 'I
don't mind. Don't be sad. It's easy.' On the bed the long
white hands had moved gently after gentle feathers,
the floating tips of the death that waited, with Helen, in
that room.

'I feel as if I've been dying of cancer all my life.' Helen
thinks now, wondering what will happen when the time
comes. Grief, like her father's grief, like her own,

already she thinks she must protect Kevin from that. Would he miss her? Would he, though? So much would continue, the children, schools, meals, music lessons, swimming baths, football, the Feis, drinks with friends, a fire in the evenings. Would he miss her smell in the bedroom, the stains her heavy periods left sometimes, her voice, her hands touching him at night, sliding under his pyjama jacket to touch with her finger the tips of his breasts, would he miss her?

It won't come as any great surprise. The sisters are the only people who still call them 'the girls'.

'One day one of us will die. It will happen. Then we'll know.' Helen looks at the surface of her own life, like her sisters' lives, and sees it as a thin membrane stretched tight over the bones. If this should be pierced by the death of one of them the rip will run right through to the heart. They will all be part of that dying.

'But perhaps it won't begin to happen until we have finished, at least with the children.' In her mind she repeats the prayer she had begun to say, so often, to the God she believes in devoutly. 'Don't let it happen until we have finished the children . . .'

Activity is the answer to all this and Helen sternly gets herself back into action. As she moves to stretch with spoons and paper napkins across the cloth her shadow touches Maura, who lies spread out uncaring, eyes closed under dense sunglasses.

The moving shadow blurs the darkness against Maura's lids and for a second only she holds an impression of something leaning above her and hiding the shielded brightness. She promises herself: 'If I open my eyes now, suddenly, it will be his face that I see.'

She opens her eyes. There is nothing, only light again. 'It doesn't matter,' Maura tells herself roughly. 'It doesn't matter.' And she banishes by listening to the sounds from the beach the shape of his head above hers, the lift of an eyebrow raised on a teasing inflection. There they are, so easily, his head, his voice, it's her own fault for bringing him here. If his smile fills her whole vision now it's nobody's fault but her own.

And anyway all that was years ago. '*Years*,' she pounds the distance into her heart. It isn't that she thinks about it much, nowadays. It's just the place really. Her own fault again, for having let him on to this family acreage. Determined self-counselling has hardened all her despairs, her emotional hull is barnacled over, she doesn't even imagine, any more, what she would do if she ever, ever, met him again.

'I don't have to waste my time imagining it. It won't ever happen,' and she turns away from the sun on to her stomach, pulling and scratching at the grass which shockingly dissolves in a mist of brimming green. That doesn't last. Maura has the kind of anger in her now that burns up tears, that makes her shake sometimes in horror at her own impatient roughness with Helen, for example, whose piety and easy sentiment seem to beg for the cruellest contradiction. She has to stop herself from rounding on Patsy, whose contentment is an inbuilt quality, and who so far has not been daunted or distracted by experience. There is something gentle in Patsy which Maura has constantly to avoid, stepping aside from it for fear of trampling it, or crushing it with her own savage reiteration of the lessons of life, of loss.

Instead she turns her cynicism into a joke for the benefit of the others, sometimes deflating Patsy's optimism, with a sour little phrase, although not without affection. 'It's for her own good,' she tells herself defensively, because she is ashamed. She doesn't say much, any more, about what she feels, what she believes.

'What do I believe?' she wonders, using the question like a hook to pull herself away from the self-pity hiding there among the grass. 'Well. I believe that life is a matter of choice, we all make choices. Maybe I call them compromises. But I keep thinking that my kind of compromise is a sordid one, while the fact is that it's only sordid because I haven't accepted it fully.'

She must accept it. She knows that, knew it when she

decided so long ago to stay married to and living with her husband. That was the only way she could stay with her children; the life she is living now is what staying with them means. A life empty of love, peppered with small disappointments, devoid of large disappointments because there are no large hopes, a life growing invulnerable to the uncertainties of her husband's absences and behaviour.

'It also means,' and her fingers tapped the grass in numerical rhythm – 'it also means the car, some independence, fairly complete control of the children, considerable freedom with them and therefore a kind of happiness, ease when he's away. His being away is a bonus too. And power. If there's no sex, and he knows I miss it, he knows he owes me, I have some power over him. I like that. It just has to be enough for me.'

It is enough, most of the time. When she doesn't think, doesn't count. But she is alone a lot, especially at night, and these are the times when choices made, decisions taken, come back again as if offering themselves for review, suggesting that maybe, maybe, there is another way if only she could see it. And when once she saw the other way, opened up by the mirth and tenderness of what Helen would have called 'an Extra-Marital Affair?' if she had known about it – well, that had again resolved itself into a matter of choices to be made.

Maura can remember the searing ease with which she decided. It is not a memory she welcomes, it is something she has battened down. But here in the sunny comfort of the afternoon her repressive energy has weakened, she realizes something of what memories are for, even memories of renunciation remind us at least that there was something to renounce. It had happened at night, she had been alone, still saturated with the bliss of physical rediscovery, still confident that the next day they would meet again, there was time. The children were in bed, the house quiet, the cat lay curled against an armchair by the fire, but she had left

87

the toys where they had been abandoned by the children in their last game of the day. She was tired, and thought with tired pleasure of a trip to Dublin, a shared hotel room, theatres, restaurants, music and complicity.

In the cosy gloom of the evening colours and shapes melted through her absorption. Some part of her consciousness must have been open to them, and to the shining red of the overturned train, the yellow plastic building blocks, the primary shapes and colours sharpened against the twilight and grew more strident. She recognized them, heard what they said. 'What about us?' they said.

'What about us?' The small insistent words had brought her back, banished the bones of what she now calls an illusion. That's what she says to herself, illusion was all that affair was, nothing. Just a sex-starved rearing of desire colouring a succession of otherwise meaningless incidents, easily dismissed when the price was quoted.

'Ah, now, that's *really* sordid,' she says now, knowing. 'That's really sordid. It's squalid, to belittle it, and him – myself even – like this. Wouldn't it be more bearable if I could let myself think that the sacrifice *was* a sacrifice, that there was something there worth giving up? Why must I degrade it?'

Degraded, it fits the contours of her own despair. It doesn't happen often now, but sometimes, on those empty afternoons when the children are still at school, Maura pleases herself in the silent bedroom, not looking at herself, not thinking of what she is doing except as a matter of pressure, tightness and release. It lasts for perhaps five seconds when it happens, and then – oh, then she feels soiled, that's when sordid means more than a word to her. It was marriage which introduced her to the press of the black lace basque under her breasts, the smell of the long black stockings, the tangle of stiletto heels in the sheets. Nothing at all is left of that now, except, sometimes, a lingering craving. But that will go, too.

'What I really want,' thinks Maura in the sunlight, 'is to be an old woman. That will make everything easier. And that will come, all I have to do is wait.' Her waiting has begun; it is still true that there is corrosive loneliness, an awareness of solitariness that makes her keep away from people, so certain is she that she is no longer like anyone she knows. Even her sisters, who think of her. But they no longer include her and Duncan, her husband, in their parties or dinners or evenings out, they know Duncan won't come and it's so awkward, a woman on her own.

So Maura is settling into a life that hardens day by day like a mould around her, conscious of her estrangement but not having the energy to fight its influence. Sometimes at night she lifts one of the sleeping children into her own bed for company, for love. Sometimes she brings the cat upstairs, and the purring quiescent body shapes itself into the bend of her knees, the feel of something warm and willing, content to be with her.

There are other nights. Nights when she stands in the doorway of the children's bedroom and tries with her brain to penetrate the density of their sleep. If she could do it then, it would be all over so easily. A pillow over the smallest face and a quick deep stab through with the meat knife, through pyjama jacket, vest, skin, and all the rest. Over. No pain, no fear, no further separation ever. Then her daughter. Pillow, knife, sleep, the end.

But she would hold them close, move them in her arms into the bigger bed where they could all be together, lie close together so that the contours of their clasped bodies would fuse into one another, so that the silent longing hug would last, so that her own body would hold their warmth even while they cooled into their final shape, so that she would not be alone while the knife slid into each wrist of her own hands and blood and sleep together would bring them to the grave. There would be no noise, no grief except her own. She could do it.

And Duncan, coming in at three o'clock in the morning, would find them all. What would he notice first? That she was not in her bed? Would there be a smell, a feeling, a special stillness in the house? What message would their three bodies leave in the silence of the air? And what would Duncan do then?

'Sick. Sick, sick, sick. I'm sick. Diseased.' And Maura jumps up, shaking the heat out of her head, moving over to help Helen, to be restored by the comforts of arrangements, sharing, appeasement. Her life is propitiation. Its shadows hold chasms of shame and misery. Maura has to try to forget them, to fight them, with sandwiches.

Patsy is already looking forward to going home to her small house outside the city where Ambrose will not be waiting for her. His absence makes the house empty in a way which suits her lazy mood of this afternoon; nothing to do here on the beach except enjoy it. Nothing to do at home except get the small boy ready for bed, read a little story, taking time, maybe a bath to get the sand out of his chubby crevices. When he's in bed she'll make herself a cup of tea, a sandwich, read the papers, and then, if the light lasts, spend an hour or so in the garden.

The garden is nice now, the new trees are fruiting for the first time, a couple of strawberry plants look promising, she can check the netting on them, cut the dead heads from the climbing rose around the tree near the gate, water the geraniums. And all for Ambrose. For the small boy too, probably, he loves to dig with her in the garden, to exclaim over worms, to pull, unless seen in time, grass, weeds and flowers together out of the soil. But even as she plans these small operations for later on, Patsy knows that their object is the reassurance of Ambrose, reminding him how securely life goes on when he's away, as he has to be away so often these days.

She does wonder, though, why this work, to be worth

doing, must deserve the acclamation of a man? Would she do it if it were simply for herself? It's not that Ambrose thinks that this is all for him, it's that she expects him to. She smiles when she discovers herself bestowing these expectations, praising herself in terms of a man's approbation. It's as though she wants him to like her more; Ambrose, whose love she trusts absolutely, to whom her generous spirit responds with buoyant fervour.

'What would it be like,' Patsy wonders now, 'if we could exist without men, like nuns, as if men were known about, but unexpected, not relevant to our daily lives?' She stretches her arms, linking her fingers, stretching them over her head and lying back against the shallow dune. 'What would it be like if we didn't know or even suspect what our sex was for, that it had any purpose outside our own small needs? And why do I feel when Ambrose isn't there, when I think of him not being there, as if half my body, no, not just my body, something more robust, my *corporation*, the whole circle of my self, why do I feel as if half at least of that had been broken clean away? That's the word for what I would feel, clean. Undisturbed.'

No babies, though. Patsy's love for her little boy is the most innocent passion she has ever experienced. If she is touched by any anguish now it is from the decision that she and Ambrose have talked about increasingly in the last few months, their chosen response to the growing need for more money. She will go back to work, she agrees she has to.

They had married young, Ambrose had been twenty-six, she had been twenty-three; they had intended to delay the baby and had managed to do so for two years. Optimistic, they thought things looked good. Ambrose had passed his final examinations, had gone on courses – he was away on another one now, when would these end? – and they felt this was a good time for a baby, and so he came. Patsy could do that, tele-scope an event into a matter of decision and fulfilment:

they had wanted a baby, a baby came. Maura laughed when she heard her talk like that, she said Patsy was the only person she knew for whom wish-fulfilment really worked.

This wish, being granted, changed the prospects of other wishes. Not that they were so important. Patsy knows that, only a matter of advances, prospects, spending power. Money had changed, the world outside themselves had grown hostile and uninhabitable. To keep the car, the house, even their hopes under their own name they needed more money more often. Without too much prompting Patsy saw that it was time for her to move back, although all her thoughts had been on going forward.

Three days a week, to start with. Helen will mind the boy until Patsy can find 'a good girl'. To pay *her* she will have to work five days a week. All change. And what about other babies? Not for years, now. The IUD suits her so well she hadn't any worries about 'mistakes' – but for how many years? And what if they get to depend on her wages? And how will the small boy feel, seeing Mummy go away every morning?

'He'll get used to it,' and Patsy reassures herself by depending on Helen's certainties – Helen wouldn't let them get away with a thing. He will learn from Helen, of course, that while some Mummies do go out to work, it's best when they don't, when they can stay at home. He will have to learn from Patsy and Ambrose that some Mummies do go out to work, that was that. And surely he will always know how very much she loves him?

By now Patsy has herself tuned to the notion of the office, the girls, the patter and the challenge. It wouldn't be easy, some girls might resent her arrival, her own independent nature might make things difficult with her employers. But already the great big worry of money seems to grow smaller as she decides what to do about it. The bigger worry of the looming good-byes elongates all her responses to her child, to

92

the other children. That will be her burden, for years to come. Still, if she is going to work, she tells herself now, she's going to do it wholeheartedly, make something of it. That's the way to do it, either that or disdain it altogether, as Helen does. It was a mistake, a bad mistake, to dabble at it, reluctantly, like Maura, taking on a commission here, a commission there. In fact, Patsy realizes, Maura hasn't done a single stroke of dedicated work since her marriage. 'Since Mammy died.' Patsy adds it up, wondering if the death, rather than the marriage, is the clue.

'It couldn't be. Maura never mentions Mammy. I remember they were close, I remember the wedding was a great day for both of them. As though they were both in love with Duncan.'

'Love.' She remembers not much else of those few remembered days, but thinking now of Angela Carter, written words, Jill Tweedie, Margaret Drabble, Shakespeare, Brian Moore. 'Ambrose will be home on Saturday. How good that will be. I love it when he's been away, we're so eager, the tenderness.' Her face burns as she lifts it like an offering to the sun. She thinks of her husband's shoulders, the blades bare under the skin, the pubic hair that flares towards his chest, hair that seems to her infatuation to be all over his body, so that the black spikes on his fingers, even when he's dressed for Mass, can lead her senses back to the feel of his ribs under her hands, to his white buttocks stretching apart for her gentle curiosity, her desire.

Thinking of him, of the things they whisper to each other in bed, of his arms around her suddenly in the kitchen, his palm on her breast under her blouse, she remembers how once she had posed for him in black knickers, standing flaunting herself in the headlights of the car parked off the road not far, in fact, from this very beach. It was winter, and cold, and she had stood only for a few freezing moments in the light, but had not felt the snow floating on to her breasts, only the pinch of her suspenders, the snap of the garter belt as she bent provocatively for his enjoyment.

That had been the most voluptuous sight of his life, he had told her years later, long long after their furious unmarried grappling on the back seat of the car had been forgotten. The most voluptuous sight of his life had been the snow falling on the black sheen of her pants, and clinging to the black stockings. It amazes her now to remember those days, those nights of desperate restraint. How had they managed to hold out so long? She thinks with a giggle of the subterfuge they had used, even with one another, to pretend that everything they were doing left her – and him too, although they didn't mention that fact – a virgin. Only in Ireland, she thinks, only in Ireland could a couple be lovers, as we were, and still be virgins.

'But that was love too,' she says to herself, wondering what other people do. She has always tried to forbid her curiosity, knowing that someday it might betray her. Once she discovered a letter her mother had kept, from her father. 'Come back soon,' he had written, 'I long for you, for your body beside me in bed, for your curly head on the pillow.' How had she found that? It must have been written such a long time ago, to be found somehow after her mother had died. 'What was I looking through? Why? I don't remember having very much to do about anything at that time. But I did see that letter, no one but myself.'

It had lain among the brown photographs in the old brown dressing-table, the piece of furniture that Patsy had loved most, been most conscious of, in her childhood home. The drawers on one side were her mother's, those on the other belonged to her father. On that side, in those drawers, were old wallets, a gold tie-pin still hanging on to cotton wool, handkerchiefs with a thin coloured border, a strong, clean leather smell, a faint tinge of tobacco, something of the smell that came from the bottom of the wardrobe in that room, where he had kept old shoes and those pale boxes with their funny, frightening gasmasks inside.

The left-hand stack of drawers had been the real fascination. These had held all the traces of her mother, tinkled with fine pink face-powder, a small porcelain pot of glossy rouge, hairpins from those days of long hair and chignons, old perfume bottles, a dried-up rose still brown as blood against a spray of rusty fern. Photographs of girls with corrugated hair and men with wide trousers, tennis-players, picnics, the letter. A love letter.

A small bit shocked at herself for reading it, the adolescent Patsy had also been shocked at this proof of her parent's otherwise hidden bodies. She can't think now what happened to the letter, what she did with it, perhaps she left everything there. 'Mammy can't have been dead for long when I found it, though. Maybe that was why I was so amazed by it. That, and because I always thought of Mammy as already old. Not young, anyway, not even a woman who ever had been young. And that must have been simply because at that time I was so young myself.'

The letter breathed youth, and passion, a rose red and vibrant against its clutching dark-green ferny stems. All it means was that her own mother and father had been young, once. 'As we are now,' thinks Patsy, getting up from her sprawl on the dune. It is time to get the baby, to bring the children up along the beach to the picnic her sisters have spread underneath the old tree.

She wanders down towards the little rocks, the sand and sea and sky swimming around her as she moves, the air leaping alive with sound as the children answer her calls. Name by name they run towards her, tossing laughter and water and sand about them as they rush. Turned to go back, surrounded by children, Patsy looks up towards the dune and sees her sisters. Their summer skirts flare around them like the tissue-paper crinolines of downturned poppies. With shrieks the older children gather speed and race to reach their mothers, who are sitting there, waiting for them. 'As young as we are now,' wonders Patsy, watching the children; 'will they remember us, like this? Or are we, too, already old?'

Long before dusk the beach is deserted. The sun slants away, the shelving sand is bare but for the dragging tide. As dusk deepens, the strand curves into a dish, in which the tree stands like a chalice. The cupped branches hold the cries not of birds but of children, vague cries suspended there until the darkness comes, then they too float away, drifting with weed and wrack towards the last of the light out on the farthest sea.

Displaced Persons

She was taking alone a journey she had hoped to share. She hadn't actually asked him to come. Instead she had just said where she had to go, how pleasant it might be, the people they could call on, Skibbereen, Kealkil, Ballydehob, Schull and Goleen, the lure of Roaring-water Bay. On his dismissal the day fell apart.

All it meant was that she would miss the pleasure places, the places she would have gone just to show him, the spilling lakes seen from the hillside, the forgotten slate quarries hidden by forest, the roads she knew, unseen from the main road, but they were there and she knew them, leading to a cottage, a castle, a dark pool set in secret heather. That was all his refusal meant. No, it also meant that he could do very well without her, even though their days were numbered now. Oh, well. Perhaps he didn't count the days the way she did; it was like going to Dublin sometimes. 'Are you up for the day?' everyone said. 'When are you going back?' Her own instinct, meeting him and recognizing him, had been the same as that: to fix the day, the time, in which she would have to be ready to let him go again. So from the beginning she had known; that was supposed to make it easier, but not easy.

Changing gear for the corner looming among great boulders she shifted in the driving seat, feeling sticky with dazzle from the windscreen. The landscape danced around her passage through it, she felt the ripples of air, the accelerator beneath her sandalled foot plunging her through the light, the heat, the day that she had longed for. The smell of leather came back to her, the hot smell of the sunny car, the slightly worrying smell of the hot engine.

'What did you say your name was?' he had said, struggling to accommodate this woman who had thrust herself – yes, she was only slightly ashamed of that, but it did come back at her sometimes, at times like this – who had thrust herself positively at him saying, 'I remember you: remember me?'

It was not possible for him to remember her. The glow began when he did not pretend; that made it easy for her to laugh, to apologize with some grace, to smooth a hollow in their encounter into which he could pour a little of his own charm. She made it plain that nothing was his fault, she had been so delighted to see him again, in Cork of all places, he need not blame himself for a second. He didn't; relieved, he had laughed too. They had formalized it, pleased with themselves. He was Kevin Murray, she was Orla Bracken, I've read so much of your . . . I've seen so much of your . . . Very pleased to meet you.

It was only the heat, and the long steady driving pressure on her arms and her right foot, only these made her feel uncomfortable now. It had not been a bad start, after all. The things she had been able to tell him about himself had pleased him. He had enjoyed being reminded, what she remembered he had forgotten, her recall amused and disarmed him, she had made sure of that. Right then, right then and there she had established that he was going back to Edinburgh within a few days, three, she had been exact. It was important, she had found long ago, to know these things. But that evening she had felt, not loose, but, well, loosed; let off, let out. It was early summer. The light was gay, the splashed poppies on her cotton frock reinforced a feeling of safe abandon, she was going among cheerful friends who expected nothing from her except her company.

She hadn't even been bored when she saw him. She

had not reached that stage of feeling she had remained too long in the same conversation. There had been easy passages among both friends and strangers, and there was no doubt about it, she had been buoyed up by some new sense of herself, an almost physical lightness. Oh, all right, and she wrenched the handbrake up to hold her against the hill while she changed into first, stupid mistake on this incline, she knew it was coming, stupid! But all right, it was true, that evening she had been happy. It was as simple as that.

The windscreen misted with tears. It had been as simple as that. She slowed, pulled in and stopped, the low hills spreading out like a badly-made bed. Not seeing them she leaned her head against the hot steering-wheel, its corrugations pressing into her forehead. With wet eyes she saw that the horn-button in the steering column had loosened with the heat; she hit it, disgustedly, and there was no sound. Still, the action and the care with which she had to replace the button revived her. The fact was this: that evening it had been quite logical to be happy. There was no point in being wistful and sentimental now about it, and if she could be tough with herself, even for a second, she would have to admit, as she wrestled with sweating hands on the steering column, she had to admit that just as she would once again have all those reasons for being legitimately and unquestionably happy, so she would once again be so. The reasons, at least, could not change for a long time.

The children and the dog had been playing all afternoon in the field behind the house. A long, intricate game, which yet made room for the assorted ages of the children of at least three families. The older boys had posted themselves on walls, with hurleys as weaponry, or hunted for stones and old branches with which to mark out boundaries. Within the boundaries the girls had played with the smaller ones, sending them on mock messages, or to bed, or to hospital where they were visited with a great deal of ceremony and some drama.

In the garden she had heard how the throb of a ship on

99

the river had brought them all rushing to the wall near the road, and the girls had used this break as an opportunity to beg for orange juice or milk or even water, and whatever broken biscuits and unimportant fruit was available. All these they took back to the field, where they ate, among the grasses, within their careful walls. She had worked away in the garden, swearing sometimes of course; some things had gone wrong, a branch had been broken from the pear tree, a football had damaged the seedling sweet pea, there would be no way at all of dealing with some of those weeds except by getting down on her hands and knees and digging them out one by one. But the new aubretia had come on wonderfully and had delighted her by encouraging the older plants, which now hung in cascades of purple along the wall.

The smallest boy had found a ladybird, and brought it, almost stumbling with care, in to her so that they could put it on a rose bush. They sat together on the hot lawn for a little while.

> Ladybird, Ladybird,
> Fly away home
> Your house is on fire,
> Your children are gone!

Several times she had to say it; he loved it, he loved being reassured that it was not really so, that the ladybird's children were safe and well and that the ladybird knew where to find them.

Tea-time had been early, distinguished by a strawberry shortcake made, she understood from the recipe, the American way. The children had enthused about it. There was enough left for the babysitter. She had been able to bathe in the comparative peace of a television programme they all liked. The sitter was one they all liked too, and when Orla came back downstairs, 'dressed up' as they loved to say, they had teased and played the game from *Young Frankenstein* – they had to beg to kiss her, to kiss her goodbye, and she had to shriek: 'Not the lips!' and 'Not the face!' and 'Not the hair!'

She left on a litany: the story to be read for the youngest, already in pyjamas; the time at which the others were a) to go to bed, and b) to stop reading. Sometime, she thought, scattering telephone numbers and the likely time of her return into whichever ear would receive the information, sometime I'll have all this written down, it will be fixed and unchangeable, sometime.

Jaunty in high heels and buoyant with petticoats she had sat into the car and the machine, catching the mood of the day, had started immediately and sweetly. Sunglasses softened the road into town, across the two rivers, up the hills to the north side, to the house, to the party, to him. It had been such a happy day.

It was too hot to sit any longer in the car. She had better keep moving. There was work to be done, people to see, arrangements to be made. When she had had to make this journey before she had thought that diving into West Cork was like driving into a hive of particularly industrious bees; they would buzz and whirr round her, offering the handwoven blankets, the hand-thrown pots, the glass, ceramics, the quilts, as though they were superior types of honey. And then, within the hive, she found cells of uncompetitive warmth, of enlightenment and kindness. She had looked forward to going back there.

Moving off, she took the usual small comforts to heart: the seat-belt strapping her to safety, the red jacket on the back seat ready against the chill of the evening, the book, and Skibbereen ahead. She would stop there and buy good things at the cake shop; something creamy for herself which she persuaded herself was enough for lunch, a currant loaf to take home, sparkling with sugar, buns and a brack for Una and the children. Una and *Daithi* and the children. Where there was resident husband, what was she doing disposing of him even mentally? She hadn't intended to visit there, at first, they weren't on her list. But she felt a need growing in her for their self-absorption; they would never assume she would not be interested in their concerns, she couldn't be bored or idle or lonely there.

Just how true this was she realized only a few hours later. She took the turn into the rutted track that led to their house above the sea before she had meant to. Losing heart in the honey of macrobiotic contentment, shaken by the thin and silent children who snatched the wheaten crumbs from her plate – she had never been able to convince herself that hunger was a healthy state – she had abandoned her main reason for making the journey at all and had turned back to the town from which the path to Una's house could be most easily reached. As she drove noisily and fearfully up, sounding the horn at each omnivorous bend, she met Daithi coming down, his car full of people and children. Of men and children, she realized, when they stopped and smiled at each other and explained themselves through the open windows. Brendan was on holidays, so was Peter, both with their children, both staying with Daithi and Una, they would all be back at the house before she left. They went on down to the village for lemonade, ice-cream and Guinness, she went on upwards.

At the house she realized they had been evicted. Una met her with wails; God was to be thanked that she hadn't brought any of her own children. There were notices up on walls, leaden with the irony that children love and that adults use as a pretence that they're not asking for anything unreasonable. Una didn't mind, she said now, being a house-mother. But surely she was entitled to the privacy of her bedroom? She laughed, but spoke as if she were trying to recognize the shape of her own life under this rubble of visitants.

To Orla she explained that Brendan was finding out whether or not he could live without his wife, who anyway, in anticipation of his conclusion, had left him. Briefly the two children had been taken to another farm

102

further up another mountain, but this, Una said, was only temporary, and Dublin was the eventual destination. In the meantime the children had been sent back down to spend some time with their father, who was not at all sure what to do with them, or with himself. Except to lodge them all with Una for a while, using the summer as an excuse.

'I feel as if this house is a clearing centre, a camp for displaced persons,' Una said, pushing Orla in front of her into the garden, where they drank tea and ate the sugared bread in a precise, deliberate ceremony, using china cups, a delicate old teapot, lemons cut with frilled edges. The sun was sinking on the hills that curled towards Mount Gabriel; immediately beneath the low wall edging the grass the rocks tumbled down to where their bits and pieces made walls for fields, small rocky fields that clung to the hillside until they became vegetable gardens, backyards, and a street that led to the glittering sea.

Listening to Una, watching her careful movements with cups and spoons, Orla thought that West Cork had its own sense of order. Wild though the landscape was, yet it fell into place; the lack of discipline in the lives of its newer inhabitants was only apparent. They lived by their own rules. And when disaster disturbed those rules they knew where to rest until new structures could be designed.

'Yes!' said Una. 'Yes. With me, with Daithi. Because we've held on to things that they abandoned when they left the cities. Not everything, obviously, but we're not so dedicated to the idea that our own rhythms are the only timekeeping we need to observe, and we do think constantly about our kids, what they're doing, what they should be doing, and we still respond to the notion of comfort in our lives – we have worked to achieve it.'

'Oh,' she sighed and moved to the garden chair, 'it's not that I mind all this. They are our friends, really, and of course I want to help. But they won't admit that their lack of order matters. Here they are now, shipwrecked to

103

all intents and purposes, and they don't even know which lifeboats are seaworthy. With such a precious cargo! The whole thing exhausts me. I'm exhausted.'

She was glad Orla had come, she was viciously glad she had pushed everyone out of the house. She wanted one small piece of this day to herself, the uncomplicating company of another female, the opportunity to grouse and grumble to someone who wouldn't be around to remind her of it. Orla knew, smiling as she thought of it, that only Una would feel the need to apologize for kicking against this situation. She knew too that the instinct of the men had been absolutely right; they had homed in to Una because in her atmosphere, in the calmness which she and Daithi maintained around their days, the various children could live without any extra anxieties.

They lazed in the garden, talking or not. They never used the word 'sad'; they knew it, that was enough. The sound of a toiling car brought Peter back; he had left the others below, he had been anxious to be there when small Petey woke up from his afternoon sleep. 'Petey', wondered Orla. That must mean that Peter and his vanished, far-away, unforgotten wife had loved one another enough, such a short time ago, to name the baby boy for his father. It was something that spoke of such expectation, 'Petey'. Now Petey had to live with their disappointment.

When he came into the garden in his father's arms the small boy did not like another new face. He turned from Orla, moping into Peter's shoulder. Peter was rallying, asking for a big-boy display of manners. Watching him doing exactly the wrong thing for the child, a child apart from his mother for a brutal month and for the first time in his life, Orla wondered at what stage Petey would realize that these months were to be the pattern of his future existence, and whether Peter, or the child's mother, would understand before then how ill-equipped they had left him, and try to change things. It was most unlikely, she thought, hearing Peter now encouraging the three-year-old to be a man. Peter spoke of him with love, but the love of a deprived person for something that he sees as unattainable. He could not have Petey for himself; for this month he tried to get everything from his son that he would long for, miss, extol, boast about in the coming year.

When Petey, contented for a while, whispered against the sea-tanned skin of his father's neck, Peter smiled and moved his hand smackingly against the seat of the small boy's jeans. Smiling too, the child slipped onto the grass and ran across the garden, his plimsolls skipping over the flower border, his bright blue T-shirt shrining the small body, the garden itself containing his bright brief image for a second after he had vanished into the shadows of the house, where he was to demonstrate his manhood to himself in the bathroom.

When Peter asked Orla how things were with her she responded with questions about what was happening to him. Things were all right, really, considering. They both knew what he had to consider, and considering it were silent. When he spoke then about his wife, Orla was dismayed to hear the venom in his voice. She had seen them together once, linked, she had thought, by a glowing, delighted love. Now Peter spoke in pounds and pence, weighting maintenance like a payment on the child's body. It was unbearable; gasping at him, laughing to hide her anguish, Orla said, 'Stop it, stop! You're talking about me, you know!' He laughed too. Perhaps for the same reason. But it was true. To someone else, to her own children's father, Orla was the paid-off wife, bartering her children's bodies like goods for money.

Getting ready to go she groped for sunglasses, handbag, the tea-tray for Una. Stepping from the sun into the flagged kitchen her foot rustled on a piece of paper, and when her hands were free she picked it up. It was a child's drawing. One of Brendan's girls, Una said, was always drawing. Quite a talented child, she said.

The picture, drawn in crayons on lined paper from a school copybook, showed a large ladybird with a headscarf and an apron, mother ladybird. Another ladybird wore only a headscarf, but carried a parcel, or perhaps a satchel, or a suitcase; something almost square, marked into quarters. Careful letters along the lines told the story:

'The Ladybird. One day the mother ladybird said to her daughter, you are big enough now to live by yourself. Pack your bag and fly away. The little ladybird packed her bag and watched her mother fly away from her, far far away, and then she flew away herself, carrying her bag. That's why when you tell a ladybird to fly away home, she doesn't know where to go. The End.'

Orla left the sheet of paper on the kitchen table. She felt like marking it 'to whom it may concern'. All her goodbyes were said, she kissed Una, laughing at her, seeing her laugh back, life would go on, they would manage. But as she buckled herself once more into the car, chasing a bewildered bee out the window, she felt as if she were dragging something from the house with her. She rejected the image of a ball and chain, of course, but it was something weighty, something that would not leave her mind alone. She had happened like an accident in that house – why did she feel its several groupings coming together to present her with a single message?

For a while she did not think at all but drove. By the time she reached Leap the sun had not yet begun to set, there was still no chill in the evening, there was no hurry on her. She turned left before Rosscarbery, a long way before, and took a thin road across a broad mountain, not knowing where it went. Where the hill crested and the road sloped again towards a dim valley she pulled in against a gateway. Up here there was a light wind, smelling of the hay in the small yellow fields. She took out her book, the buns, the apple, and began to read and to eat. But the thrill of guilty surprise which disturbed the amateur theatricals at Mansfield Park on the famously inopportune return of Sir Thomas failed her for once. She could not eat without words before her eyes, and putting both book and cake aside she got out of the car and walked a little way along the path.

How sweet the fields could smell, how gentle the colours on the evening hills above them; a bird sang his last song of the day, and she knelt into the clovered grasses of the meadow beyond the ditch, digging her knees into the yielding pasture and then lying her body into it, nothing around her at all but the grass stirred by her own pressure on it. And how she longed for him. Forget, she told herself, forget that he might not feel like this, forget that life is not earth for him, nor growth goodness. The heat of the land she lay on swelled back to her, and thinking of him, of his white body when they were last together, a surge of liquid warmth filled her with such grief that she turned her head into the pillowing grass and wept.

At their second meeting she had meant it to happen, she had brought her diaphragm with her, the pessaries. She had meant it, she must have meant it. But it had been he who asked. She had been delighted to agree. It was good, after all, to wait until opportunities like this came. She had not hungered for sex before this; a long abstinence had whittled her desire to something thin and frail. Now, oh now as their bodies parted at last on that flower-spread bed, now she knew that she was condemned to appetite, to hunger.

It had happened, for all that, so quickly. The question asked, the answer given, they had returned to the hotel room and stood looking at each other inside the door. They had both laughed at the same instant, at the realization that all the necessary preliminaries had already been observed, that all that was waiting for them was to love one another. Weaving between the sheets in grateful exploration she had recognized the delicacy of his approach, the advent of his body on hers was not aggressive or demanding. Her body was grateful, grateful and amazed. His was more subtle, almost shy, and seeing this her hunger was held back. Held back, but it filled her so that her mind was a dam

107

against its insistent tide. It blocked her ears to what he said, to what he meant beyond the words.

'I hope you won't fall in love with me,' he said, and she had smiled. First at this gentle arrogance, the assumption itself seemed funny to her. Then at the fact that she did not, after all, feel what she could call love. Was it possible, she wondered, to fall in lust with somebody? What she had not done was question him. And weeks later, when he had returned to the city and called her, she had not questioned him then, either. She had been insatiable, there was no time. She poured over his body, her own by now – the weeks of absence and distance had made sure of this – by now too full, too blown, too old, to be important.

She had gone to him then feeling blessed. Something she had been dreading had taken place. Not this absence. She had not feared that then, although now she did. No, it had been the threat of another absence, the children were to go to stay for a week with their father. The week selected, the arrangements made, they had gone. She was blank with surprise at its painlessness.

Before inviting him to it, she had looked at her house, wondering how it would hold him, what he would think. But when she did ask him he had asked instead, 'Will your children like me?' What an odd question, she had thought. Relieved, licensed, she had said that they wouldn't be there, and thought no more of that. What had stopped her then, why had she not explained, let him into her own life, instead of just saying that they were away, on holidays? And oh, how she had wrung the muscles of her heart since then, searching for the reason why she had not listened to him, had not noticed that he too was seeking the sound of children's voices.

Ah, she thought as she moved in the grass, turning so that once again she looked up at the sky that was now growing dull, she had not asked these questions because she did not want him to know about her, about her children gone for a court-certified week with their banished father, about her children for whom some other woman was now caring, complaining in a mild undemanding way.

It was dusk. Something swift, long and brown leaped away from her feet as she climbed over the ditch; startled for a second, her next thought was that Betsy would know what it was, that she would tell Betsy about the small animal in the slumbering hay. Betsy, whose grave little face had shone at her over the back seat of their father's car, eager for the journey but sorry to leave, whose look then and so often these days reminded her of the line from Patrick Kavanagh, 'smiling at me with violets'. When it was spring again they would search for violets together, and primroses, and note those which they might later transplant to Betsy's own little patch in the back garden. Those days were not so far away, now, after all.

She thought, on that thought relying on next spring. One day I will be surprised to realize that this all happened a year ago. It was a little bit like having a baby; you had to get through this contraction, because the next one might be worse. She had to get through this day, tomorrow would be worse.

It had happened already that it had turned out worse. All that time he had been away, the time after their first few meetings, she had wished with shame for solitariness. The children had hummed like flies among the heat of her obsession. When they were gone, and she was free, and he had come back, within a day or two it had faded into this emptiness.

She heard his voice above her hair. 'Use your muscles,' he had whispered fiercely at her. Those were the muscles which had ripped apart on the exploding birth of one of her children. She had used them once and after that there was nothing left to use. She could not tell him that. She had wanted briefly to try, but then knew better. She shrank, folding herself limp and still, grief creeping into every crevice of her closing body.

Well, in time, she told herself, putting the car in gear, moving into and down the rutted track, driving into the looming dark, in time I will forget those words too. I will forget that last meeting, the dinner-table, candles and wine, the official 'thank you' meal. He was so polite, so courteous, and so distant, while there seemed to be no language left for her but touch. But if she had reached for him he would know everything. She did not move towards him, he did not ask her to. She left. It was over.

Driving home, across the luminous causeway at Rosscarbery, she was travelling towards a still empty house. She thought of the children, away in someone else's home, learning what it was to be displaced persons. When you peel an apple, she thought, the flesh comes as no surprise; although so different from the skin it is only what we are accustomed to find. If she peeled the skin of love from the children's lives, what would she find, now that she no longer knew what to expect?

A Way of Life

The hall door shut with a satisfied slam behind her. The rooms empty of children gaped on the landing but the house was warmly ready for her, her sounds and movements animating it as she completed the small rituals of night, the patina of her contentment glazing the waiting air of her bedroom, where books took up the space of another body.

In the chilled mirrors of the bathroom she watched with equanimity the reduction to self, safe here where she was known so well, but not to be feared even elsewhere, when so often as again tonight the texture of her own skin surprised and pleased her, and the thick untinted hair denied years she did not otherwise deny. It was happening: she plucked out a coiled grey hair, and sighed at the trace of blood on the toothbrush.

'I have reached an age,' she reminded herself, 'where it is important that my dentist does not die before I do.' But even this reflection could not dim the glow of tired elation with which she prepared for solitary sleep.

'Don't you just *adore* men?' Peggy had asked her once. They were standing together watching a young and hungry barrister spur the gravel of Peggy's Dublin South avenue as he turned his battered sports-car. 'I do. I just adore them. They're so – *innocent*. So, after everything, so easily pleased.'

Smiling, Anna had wondered again about Peggy. Safe in a marriage which by all Irish standards must be called good, with a wealthy man who didn't drink, didn't smoke, didn't play golf, whose most obvious assertion was his undramatic fondness for Peggy herself, she and her husband were a tanned and thriving couple with a yacht, a house by the sea, children at famous monastic schools, and government ministers to dinner even when their government was no longer in power.

With it all there remained, perhaps essential to Peggy's attractiveness, a trace of raciness, a strange wild flavour to the well-managed life.

'No,' Anna said. 'I'm still afraid of them. They own too much, they can do such damage.' Stephanotis arched above its own reflection on the laquered table in the hall where they still stood, still gazing at the shredded gravel before the steps. As Peggy put her hand to the vaulted door, Anna saw the heavy gems on the thin, elegant wrist and recognized Peggy's smile, a smile tinged with remembered satisfactions.

'No,' Anna said again. 'There is nothing that they have that I want. Now.'

Peggy laughed a challenge to the lie. The house made them graceful as they wandered back to the exquisite drawing room, the facets of the chandelier sprinkling light across the pastel ceiling, a green glow coming in from the extravagant city garden beneath the windows. To Anna it looked like an arrival point, and she knew that once they would have sat together in the kitchen, where dark old woods shone against old tiles and cracked ceramics fielded from deputations to the EEC had no comment to make except that of surprised survival.

Even for these conversations, talk about men, they would have sat in the kitchen. They would have wondered what had happened, how it was that they had never thought they would find themselves like this, describing to one another the minutiae of love, or at least of love-making, of their lives with men in them. In the drawing room there was no giddy wonderment; the room said it all. This was what had happened, at least to Peggy. Peggy's wealth also gave her an immunity, an equality impossible for others. She could afford, thought Anna meanly, to be generous.

The truth was that Peggy's real practical love was for her husband and family. For the rest it was a matter of emotive energy, cast over anyone who interested her, whom she could help, who attracted her. It was the only thing about her that Anna longed to emulate, that gift of generosity without fear. Admitting it to herself, Anna resorted to one of her stand-by consolations: all this talk about men, she thought, and if I mentioned Henry James she'd wonder where she might meet him!

All the same, Peggy could surprise her.

'How is it we can talk like this,' she said as they curled again into the peacocked armchairs, 'how is it that we, you and I, have no moral anxiety about our sexual lives? About what we want?'

It was nice of her to include herself, technically blameless as she was. But that was Peggy, too. There was something she wanted to say, or to find out, and she could only do it by appearing to talk of something, or someone, else. Look at the time it had taken Anna to realize that Peggy had guessed long before that something was wrong with Anna's own marriage. All those days Anna had spent with her, 'getting a break from the kids'. Those had been getting a break from the husband as well, although Peggy had never hinted at that, treating instead the worried, hurried confidences with a tact and gentleness which had appeased the gnawing anger. And then when it happened that Anna's marriage had become the conversation piece of many people Peggy had offered, characteristically at once, shelter, money, advice, throwing a rope of robust clichés for Anna to clutch, accepting without argument Anna's own imperatives, substituting her own only where Anna could not reach.

In the long calm after that long storm, Anna had redesigned her life, not skilfully, but with growing wonder at how it could all be done, almost easily, once she had accepted that there was no need, any more, to apologize. That dispensation was what made sense of her life now; learning to function without blaming anyone, she less and less blamed herself. The children had become the circumstance of her life, rather than the excuse for its deficiencies. She had grasped what remained to her and added to it, emerging, she felt sure, back where she should have started, had she only known the way.

But when Peggy had wondered, like that, out loud, Anna had been surprised.

'How is it? Peggy – you know how it is! I can talk like this, I can behave like this, because I know I'm going to pay for it. There's no need to feel guilty – retribution is just around the corner!'

She meant it, but they were both laughing. They knew how it was, everything, *everything* was paid for.

'*Everything!*' Anna couldn't stop. 'Look at this weekend – first thing before I leave at all, £19 at the Family Planning Clinic! And then the train, and taxis, and the hotel . . .'

Peggy didn't prompt her. The hotel.

'Well,' Anna had quietened. 'The hotel. That's it, really. That makes it worth the trouble, not the expense, the secrecy is the trouble, but it's worth it.'

There was a brightness in Peggy's eyes. She knew how it could be worth it, that secret, precious excitement, that breathlessness produced by nothing else at all.

'But you're still afraid of men!' She pounced. 'You don't trust them. You don't trust him.'

Of course Anna didn't trust him. How could she? She was in love with him. She had been almost sick with it, and Peggy had noticed, without saying anything more.

It had been love, hadn't it? That ripening?

This was not a question she could take to sleep with her now. How could she admit it had been love? If she gave that much she would be like a cat crouching before an empty hearth because once it had known warmth there, all the rest of her life she would be sitting not before the shrine, but before the source.

It must be that this was what she did not trust, her own sense that in themselves men held a key to a door which would open on an inner life, golden and strong, unthreatened because it was of their own essence. To be in love, if she could look at it now, was to hold the other hand of the hand that held the key, by all one's actions to encourage that key to turn, to open, to bring one in.

She had been right, Anna knew it, in what she had said those years ago to Peggy. Whatever she got, whatever she enjoyed, she would pay for, and had she but known it then, had already begun to pay. Because it had been love, an offering of small perfections which she had disclaimed. She had wanted lightness, ease, the delicacies of sexual rather than any deeper understanding, all kept possible by courtesy. And surely she was only being modern, being careful, in putting herself, politely, first?

Taking those pleasures in a Dublin city with the sun on it, in a London glittering with frost, she had said 'darling' carefully. She had not let him know how surprised she had been that he had found her out, had bothered with her, how every telephone call between them was weighed with wonderment, and if sometimes her voice betrayed her she pretended it was another excitement altogether. Only in bed did she betray her gratitude, where the unspoken love broke to a shouted lovely, where enthusiasm was permitted and could be used as a disguise.

It was good. So good as to be enough, for her. There had been traces of needs to be met which had frightened her, she had seen bleak anxieties behind the gaiety of passion in his eyes. Now that she was secure at last in her womanhood she might have found room for them, but then – then they were auguries of too much, portents which would bring her back, not forward, to before her new beginning. She was living now the new life she had protected then, and here in her own bed, in her own house, there was no longer any need to lie.

'It's not much, though, is it?' he had asked once. 'As a way of life, I mean?'

They were planning, not for the future, but for next week. They had walked a little way downhill from the car to where a brown stream tumbled over stones, and a bank of grass hid them from the road. As the September evening cooled, their serenity broke on the knowledge of parting, coming within an hour or so as the light faded down. They felt the feather of winter brush their skin, and she thought not of the rushing prance against the cold air of the beach, and the casserole in the borrowed kitchen of a friend, and the regular, regulated warmth of hotel bedrooms, but of babysitters, and money, and the lonely, lonely lack of opportunity.

What had he thought of it? Not much, he had said, not much as a way of life. It had not hurt, because he was saying that there was more on offer. Another new start, this time with him. The two children were young enough to take the change, to enjoy it. Could she? The short answer was no. There was no long answer.

'Anna!' Peggy had exclaimed. 'That was too easy! You liked him, you know you did – why not wait a little longer, give it a chance?'

'If I wait it will get harder.'

'But that would mean that you really care for him! That would make the decision for you, you would know what was right!'

'I don't want to need anyone so badly that I would change everything for him, all I have built up in the last few years. I can live without him – and he without me.'

'Yes.' Peggy's voice was subdued. 'I'm sure you can. You can live without him – but do you want to? It will be such a loss to you, Anna, you will always wonder if you could have done things differently.'

'But I wonder about that already.' Anna knew her defences were meagre. 'It's all right for you, Peggy. You're safe. But you want me to feel pain, to do it all properly, to suffer, to put values on things so that they become important to me, too important to lose, even

116

though I know I'm going to lose them. It's a price I won't pay, Peg, I can't afford it.'

When had she decided that the loss was inevitable? It didn't matter now, for it was, it was. The knowledge had governed her life since then, intensifying her relationship with Peggy for they both knew by now that of all friendships, that between themselves as women was the one which would last.

The cat had come in her window and jumped on the bed, kneading the quilt before curling into a complacent ball. The facts of her life settled down again into Anna's mind as she reached to switch off the light, smiling as she thought at last that she could say, like Peggy, that she loved men. And mean it, in almost the same way.

Before she turned into sleep she thought of him, tonight's man. Nice, and nicer because he hadn't really understood from the beginning what she had intended. That their meeting had not been accidental, that she had designed their re-discovery of a mild affection in the past, the cautious flirtatiousness of durable colleagues. As a result she could almost despise him for the ease with which it worked, but although she enjoyed that feeling of mild contempt, a dividend on the perceived disdain on boys' faces long ago at rugby dances, the boat club, although now she could feel she was paying them out, this time, with this one, she didn't.

To meet for a chat was easy, mutual concerns gave plenty of excuses. To prolong that into another drink, a break from the in-house training scheme, on to anxious thoughts about a teenager at home and thence, in a skilful elision, to a sighed reference to the wife, why, that gave room for the touch on the sleeve, the reflection that it was so nice to talk, to really talk, and to the open suggestion that they should do so again.

Lamplit in Kinsale, she had let the silences fill themselves with meaning. There had been, usually there was, a little furtive laughter, a sense of light complicity.

117

On a smile his hand touched hers and as their reminiscing allowed her to mention a lover of the past he grew bolder and his fingers touched her wrist and moved again until they touched the pulse inside her elbow, and she stirred. Then – The Look. And The Question.

Her gaze held his, steady, bright, and sober. Finishing the meal quickly he paid and put her in the car and drove up the hill to the dark pile of the fort where the walls shrouded the cliff with shadows. Unheard beneath them the confident sea pounded against the rocks, and knowing the beat of the waves down there and the surge of the wind blowing their spray against the small cage of the car, she felt again the answering rhythm within herself, the rising response. And she liked to think about it afterwards, the way he had unclasped the seat-belt and taken her authoritatively into his arms.

She looked at him again, showing him that she was deliberately studying his features, that his face mattered to her. He was only a few years older than herself, but at this time in their lives it mattered to be found attractive. He was big, greying, one of those men who become handsome before they fall into age, easily pleasant.

Leaning across to kiss him, she made it gentle, inquisitive but not demanding. The demand must be his, and as their mouths touched he brought his hands up to her head to hold her while he kissed her firmly back and deepened the kiss so that his tongue pushed past her teeth and swelled against the ribs of her throat. So. He meant it. The knowledge gave freedom to the little flick of excitement beneath her stomach and she broke from him, breathless.

'Don't you want to?' Surprise hid the beginnings of anger.

'Yes.' She put her face against his cheek, her voice pitched between a laugh and a groan. This was to be regretful desire. 'I want to. But not here, we'd have to stop. And I want to be with you, really *with* you.'

He understood her, and she knew the next question.

118

'Where?' Little boy lost.

The second question came as she directed him to the flat she was minding for a friend.

'Do you have something . . . you know? In case . . .?'

She had something, he need not worry about that. But she knew there were other moments of worry for him, although the normality of the flat, its casual comforts, the books and stereo, television and telephone, red wine in the kitchen, all these indications of a steady way of life reassured him that the growing feeling of a strangeness to all this could be dismissed.

In the bathroom she wondered, she always did, if he thought about what she might be doing in there, the intimate preparations for his coming. She did not change her clothes, this was to be an honest exchange between adults, not a seduction. There was a contentment in consent, she thought, but when she went back to the living room he looked nervous again. Now what would it be – his wife? Apprehension that his performance would be unmanly or inadequate? The well-founded suspicion that he was here less of his own will than of hers?

This time it was the secrecy problem.

'This will be just between us, Anna, okay?'

It was dangerous to joke about it, so she didn't tell him that she was going to write to the papers. She was willing to draw the plot around her as though accepting his protection, of course it would be just between them. And at least his hesitation meant also that she didn't have to worry about the possibility that he was one of those men who can't accommodate their own peccadilloes, who can't sleep peacefully until their wife knows all, so that she is the one to stay awake night after night.

'Yes, please, just between us,' and she came close to him, raising her arms to his neck, lifting her face so that their coming together began with this purposeful gesture and did not end until they melted away from one another, damply pleased and close with goodwill. The

119

next few moments were often tricky, a time of satisfaction but of separation as well.

'Oh, Jesus, Anna, that was great,' he breathed at last, stirring to the other side of the mattress. He was kind: one hand stretched towards her, his fingers feathering along her side. And he had taken care of her, been diligent once he had forgotten to be amazed. No next time, though. He might want to feel himself in love, and he couldn't afford it.

Gently, absently, kissing his shoulder she whispered that she would have to go soon. She could feel him grow tense with the dilemma: how would he say goodbye without offering another date, but at the same time without appearing to be a louse? It was important to them, men, not to seem to be a louse. And he wasn't. She would do all that for him.

'Friends?' That was the note for the future. Gratefully he took it, and they dressed in accepting compatibility, were easily silent as he drove her home, and the few words at her door allowed him to relax in the knowledge that there was no blame, no expectation, nothing, ever, to disturb his own feeling that he was, after all, a nice guy.

She hoped, now, that she would remember who he was the next time they met, wherever that would be. She was going to have to slow down soon, her stage was small and the cast list was diminishing. Once, only once, Peggy had said: 'Anna, when I see you sometimes, I am afraid of the future.'

'So am I,' Anna had answered. 'And I'm living in it.'

I am, she thought now, lying at her ease. This is my future. My way of life.

For a second the children clung to the edges of her mind, their return tomorrow a thing settled and certain, the spaces they would fill unchallenged by any other claim. But because she still felt, would it always be like this? She still felt some need for an approval beyond theirs, beyond the best that they could ever offer, she led herself to sleep on the remembered choke

120

in his breath when they had first felt, naked, each other's secret skin.

She slept, and dreamed of grief. Through suburbs incandescent with laburnum she walked with long hair, lacings of gold holding a dress with pointed sleeves, a weight of paint on her lips. Trees hung lilac shadows which moved at her step and whispered 'not here, not here'. Hair grew heavy across her shoulders, her feet in thin slippers left patches of silken damp on the cobbles roughening beneath them. The bright tapestry of her gown unravelled, colours slithering as though silent remorseless hands were taking in the threads. The sky lowered, black roofs of empty houses held up the clouds, the air was light and cold, leaves blew brown from the garden walls.

The skin of her mouth cracked, the pain withered into wrinkles, in her thin hands she held a muscle which dripped red on to her bleeding feet. A shadow became a man, it was he, the one whose smile meant life to her, but the shadow turned aside, a cloak shielding his face as in a picture – where? From the flow of his hair, the line of his tunic, the delineation her vision traced of all his form could be, she knew that this was he. A cape of silk eddied against the wall as he stroked past her, so near she held out her hand in trailing rags to touch, but he was gone. In her palm she held a piece of greenish metal, a coin on which her tears fell at last.

She woke to the pain of it. Dawn and bird song, a mist filling the hills across the river.

Her hands clenched the bleached linen of the sheet, clutched grief through the fabric of her life, and she came awake to the gasping sigh with which some recognition, some knowledge of meaning, drifted past her mind.

Passing the Curragh

Once the excitement of these journeys had been the glimpse, on early summer mornings, of a string of jockeys or stable boys riding over the curved downs, a moving frieze against the sky of pearl. It would still be so; that feeling had not been replaced, only, for a while, eclipsed, as though a slow shutter had been drawn across a picture in a book, leaving it still there although hidden temporarily.

The journey home was always different to the journey down: down was when she could think of the tremble in his voice, the stutter when he answered the telephone that told him of her coming. What a delicious thing that had been to think of, her reward for ringing him once, brazenly, at his committee rooms, where she heard his throttled delight against the hum of a conversation alien to her. It was as though his voice had flushed.

They had not done publicly dangerous things; that call, perhaps, had been the most daring. He had not been angry, either, although when they decided that she should never do it again he had been suddenly, thrillingly, implacable. She had liked that, wrongly. She had liked to see his face set, stern, even against her, a hint of something she could not control.

One can take that sort of thing a bit too far. A friend had once described the horse-riding they did as the perfect experience of middle age – excitement without danger. She had thought that was true too of his love, but something about the saying when she applied it to themselves rang too close to that contemporary proverb – power without responsibility. She had the power to move him, he had power over her, absolute power it seemed sometimes, a fierce compelling insistence to which she had to succumb – but neither of them was responsible to each other.

'If I say I love you, don't panic,' she warned after only a few weeks.

'It's only because when you bring me so close I can't help it, I do feel love, the words come to my lips and I might say them. But I can't help it.'

He had taken off his glasses and looked at her mistily. A smile gleamed beneath the fringe of his beard.

'I won't panic,' he whispered, 'not now anyway.'

After all, what had she felt when she had been run away with, when a fresh cob pretended fright and danced himself into a frenzy before taking control of the bit and bolting? The first heart-clattering seconds scared her because she was trying to anticipate the horse, to adjust so that she could ride. Once the unswerving gallop began, towards either doom or deliverance – what had she felt then as the fields raced past, her cheek on the animal's neck in an attempt to avoid branches and briars? Exhilaration. It still came back to her, that wild passion of being, a sensation almost exalted in its absolution from restraint. A succession of small ditches had calmed the creature, and they had come back to earth in a pool-strewn stretch of bog, the two of them sweating, exhausted, shaken, but not unhappy.

In her first passion of the love from which the train was rushing her away her mind had deliberated words for what she was feeling. The geography which separated them had imposed its own calm, and in those spaces she played with similes, not without despair. For if there was no word for what was happening, no word for the absolute consummation of being in being or spirit by spirit which her soul seemed to drive towards, then how could it ever be achieved, or last?

It was actuality, not metaphor, which provided the insight as when on that one crystal morning she had let her control slip through the bridle and the horse had run. That had been two bodies, two animals in flight, hardly earth-bound, so intensely rapid in their joined passage along the land that it was as if they were transparent, as if the light shone through them.

Inflamed with light she knew that what happened there in the fields was a kind of love, a passion for the smitten earth, for the torn hedges, a fleshy beneficence thundering through the ribbed extended body between her knees, under her hands, a delighted welcome for the wind blowing because it was blowing, and blowing with itself the white mane like a mist into her eyes. Seeing the menace of a swooping tree looming ahead she lay low along the horse's neck and breathed as if through his nostrils, if she were breathing, and the sweet damp of his sweat moistened her whole mind until the only words were Browning's' – 'Who knows but the world may end tonight?'

Resting, stilled at last, they had stickily begun the business of reassuming their proper selves, the animal trembling and lathered, she herself the rider again, gasping calming consoling words but reluctant to change this symbiosis, this flesh on flesh feeling of being subsumed.

I might have been killed, she thought as they walked carefully back to the stables. I might never have seen him again, I could be dead.

It would have been worth it. She could not look for that danger, she told herself so, although there was some pride for her horsemanship that she had not been thrown or hurt. But Death – that would have been absolute too. Annihilation could be another word for absorption, and as she rode towards home in the sweetness of the morning that was still there, would still be there even if she could not ride, she thought she could almost welcome it.

In a profession of words she later saw that metaphors

stretch unwillingly into truth. Like Death; not corporeal, yet insisting on the body's compliance, and an easy death at that, at a stroke, like beheading, but with every subsequent slithering of tissue into decomposition felt in all its minute intimacy. As if capillaries could burn, teeth fray, glands melt slowly in the box of her body, suppuration flood under the knuckles and joints and buckle the helpless bones into rictus.

'I died in joy,' she could say to her flaking skin. Decapitated. Appropriate enough, after all. Now that it was all over, when she had to talk to him it was as if she had no mouth, no head from which to speak. Perhaps, and she had heard it could be so, the greatest sensation of death was surprise. She would have been surprised, would she, if that horse had thrown her finally free and her fragile vertebrae had split against a tree – would she?

It had not felt like that. Back in the stableyard the surprise was that she was not dead. 'I nearly died,' a groom said, 'when I saw him galloping off with you. I thought one or the other of you would never come back alive.' And there was the surprise of her joy, so thick in her lungs that she could not breathe to reassure the others whom she had left so far behind, her mouth and head were still full of the air that had inflated her being.

Therein must have lain the clue to her future – what was that from Browning? 'Past hopes already lay behind . . .' Not that, so much as the fear that future hopes might lie behind. Not even that, but more:

What hand and brain went ever paired?
What heart alike conceived and dared?
What act proved all its thought had been?
What will but felt the fleshly screen?

Indeed as the poet said, one must have a bliss to die with.

She was not morose. It was the way things had happened, she had even made them happen. And she had

125

already had a bliss to die with when he walked into her islanded office space with his reputation, his glamour, and his ready acceptance of her as a colleague.

Her working life was all on file, and they went to find it together, and read it in a quick consanguinity of mood which she later recognized as an act of self-betrayal. The first. She should have remained more curious, not about him, but about what he could do with her job, her profession, how he would assess her. But she had never been challenged in what, over a few years, she had made her own, a speciality no one else in the newspaper had taken seriously until a couple of her articles had led to questions in parliament. She could laugh as she said that social morality was never enough, there had to be some political tint to colour anything that was to be given significant editorial space. At last, but she didn't notice it soon enough, she had achieved envy. Others thought they could do better what she, after all, had done first.

When the suggested, accepted move came it came as what in other professions would be called promotion, and not sideways, although away.

'Is this your idea?' She had not been afraid to ask, ready to be happy if it had been.

'No,' he said, 'but I do agree with it. I think it's time you moved on a bit, you're too young to be identified with only one line of work, and that whole area needs to be opened up.' She was wise enough to have hedged her acceptance with a time-limit, with guarantees. She did have ambition, but believed that success was still something to be measured privately.

Introducing him to her ideas she had felt something of his distance from her, and some erring instinct to bridge this gap led her to accept his offer of drinks, a meal, to talk. She was long enough in the game too to know that this must mean there had been discussion already, that the senior editors were talking about her job.

Not just that: an offer was being made.

'Starting a service from Dublin? Actually starting it, that kind of responsibility, setting the whole thing up?' She was amazed.

'You know we've been talking about it for a while. Our stringers have been doing well, but we must have people on the ground there now, a presence. And a location. You'd be good at it – wouldn't you?'

She knew he was right about that. She could do it, certainly. She already had status, expertise, judgement. She could have listed her attributes as readily as he did, but it was a luxury to hear them coming from him, to hear herself so accurately estimated.

'We provide the flat for you, we've got office space picked out, a telex line, and you can pick and choose about photographers. You'll have a secretary, and a budget which should allow you to use a freelance reporter. You'll have independence and flexibility and we'll be backing you down here.'

'You will,' she couldn't help laughing at him, 'until something goes wrong – and it will go wrong. Will you still back me, then?'

He reassured her with wine and, relieved, flattered, too excited by the proposition to wonder then why some of the younger men on the staff had not been picked for the job, she relaxed into confidence.

'I was beginning to wonder what I'd do with myself from now on,' she admitted. 'It can be comfortable, being Louise Duffy in a place like this. I knew I was going to have to move on, soon.'

'I don't even wait for that feeling; I move as soon as I can see the place I want to get to.' There was something abrasive, abrupt, in his way of speaking which gave her a warming sense of sharing his restlessness.

'So why is Dan Hackett still here? It's been a couple of years, hasn't it?'

'Ah, yes, and a couple of jobs too. There are reasons – and I've discovered that sometimes you can be where you want to be, only too soon.' He was telling her he was going to be editor.

She started laughing again. 'It's so sad, Dan, to see you disqualified by age.'

They laughed together, and he expanded into talk of cars, fast and sleek, and she more slowly admitted to her love of horses, less fast, but more sleek.

'My wife rides,' he said then. But she knew that already.

'And the children?' Yes, the children too rode regularly, although so far he had resisted pleas for a pony of their own.

'Only a matter of time, though,' he said. 'Every time I mention changing the car at home I'm reminded of the importance of a tow-bar. I don't like the sound of it, it has a Thelwell flavour.'

Although softened by wine, she was not dull.

'And that must be another of the reasons why you've stayed so long in this one place – the family? You're getting trapped into rooting.'

'Is that what it looks like, to you?' The spare lines of his face grew tighter, his eyes held her sharply.

'People like you, Louise,' – he spoke slowly – 'people like you don't understand how quickly life re-establishes itself with nothing more changed than what you want to be different. I understand that. I know how to do it, and I can do it anytime it suits me.'

He drank more wine, ordered brandies.

'I know when the stage is too small for me, and I know, I had to learn, how to distinguish the single important thing. The single most important thing to me. And when I see that, I figure out how to go and get it.'

She sat back from him across the table, but he leaned after her, his chin reflecting, like a long-ago buttercup, the glow of the little lamp between them.

'If you were to buy a horse—'

'Hire it,' she interjected in protest, did he know how much they cost?

'—Hire it, then. If you were to hire a horse, you would decide what you wanted it for, wouldn't you, and you would then decide on the single most important thing about that animal for you. I think life is like that, we're only renting a space, and we've got to distinguish what is the most important thing to put in that space.'

She had not said anything about her own restlessness, why she was additionally ready to move, to change, to get away.

'Horses aren't like that. I mean there is no one single thing. And anyway I think, for me at least, there's an element of romance, an excitement of dealing or living with something bigger than yourself, unpredictable, something wild, in fact, a brute being. There's a breathlessness in that which I value. So you can't pick one single thing.'

'Except that, perhaps. The wild.'

'Perhaps.' She was silent. He was going to speak, but she said—

'And not cars, either. There isn't, surely, one single thing above everything else?'

'Oh yes, there is.' There was a bright certainty in his eyes. 'Yes. Can't you guess it? *Speed.*'

She had been going to protest, to ask what if it was a person, one single person, irreplaceable, more important than all. But she said nothing, feeling suddenly convinced that if she did speak, if she did offer such a proposition, he would deny it, he would say that no such person could, or did exist.

'*Speed!*' he said. 'Imposing my pace on the world, racing through it. In a car, that's what I want.'

'You're talking about power,' she said, and he agreed, smiling as they said goodnight.

'Of course I am, Louise. Of course I am.'

Dublin suited her, and the work, as she explored it, produced a buoyancy of spirit which protected her from the despondency of occasional failures, oversights, omissions.

'Don't ask me how I could have been so stupid,' she said on the telephone one morning, anticipating the questions of the long-distance editorial conference.

'I'm as capable of being that stupid as anyone else is' – and heard him laugh at the other end of the line.

'Well,' he responded, 'I may as well tell you that there is a general review on the agenda. I know –' he wouldn't let himself be interrupted by her protest – 'I know it's before time, but I can tell you now it won't be unfavourable.'

As she drew a long breath, he added – 'Don't relax yet; nothing is confirmed, nothing is for certain. But you can take it that the feeling here is on your side.'

What he didn't tell her about was the proposal to send another reporter up to the new office. For Louise the joy of her new domain had been its apparent indivisibility; she worked alone, employing help on her own terms when she needed it. Solitariness suited her. She had not had to reveal why she had been so willing to move, to change; it had been a matter of getting away from a man. Men were everywhere in the world of her work, and had no other potency in that context. But this man had been outside that world, safely settled in another, loving her in his way, 'cut-price', she had said, wanting to marry her as half of what she thought she was.

'I don't know why it is,' she had flung at him in their final accusations, 'but the history of literature is full of school-masters ready to take something on the cheap, unable to live with the full value of what they might possess.'

He had not wanted a working wife, a woman with a life beyond his, an income independent of his; yet he had thought he wanted her, and she had felt some equalizing allure in what he had to offer. It made her ashamed. It made her anxious to get away from him too, because there was a frequency of accident in their encounters which kept on resolving into little oases of consolation for them both, both of them seeing the parting ahead, both anxious to meet it without acrimony, and with some understanding.

She thought she understood: 'You want Dickensian

130

felicity at home, Sanderson wall-paper, Sunday lunches with your mother, camping holidays in France, and me writing garden notes for the woman's page. All that won't flow from the simple fact that we enjoy going to bed together – and anyway it isn't even the first part of what I want.'

Ah, but as he asked her, smilingly, with a kind of knowing pity, what *did* she want? She was not able to explain – 'I know it only by what it is not. Or by its quality – a sense of being good at something, by myself, being the best at it even, taking risks for it. Yes, defining myself through it, and I know for some that's failure. I'm sorry.'

It was easier to be sorry on her own, and away from him and their shared associations. She did not intend to stay away for ever. She had known even then that her life would change again, but she had never become skilful at recognizing the auguries of change.

'This doesn't change anything for you, Louise.' Dan had been given the task of explaining the new developments to her. 'Peter's job will be to work for you, to help you to expand the service you're already giving us. You should be very flattered, really, that we're sending additional staff after so short a time, before the trial period is up. It means you've convinced everyone here that we need to invest in that office, you've done a very good job.'

She wanted to keep on doing it. She tried to insist on specifications, devices to muffle the edges of her responsibility so that she could work equably with a colleague of equal status. What she saw quickly, in the new situation, was his assumption of permanence; the house in a suburb, the inquiries about schools, recreation, the search for a job for his wife, the office car.

Dan came up to explain it to her.

'What we're doing here, Louise, is we're building on the foundations you've established. This is your territory, don't make any mistake about that. But what we want from you now is more editorial, more decisions

131

about coverage rather then coverage itself, more comment. It's what you should be at now; what you should be doing.'

'Dan – if I'm providing, and in charge of, Dublin editorial, why won't I be called the Dublin editor? It seems to follow from what you're saying.'

He knew she could be accurate in her perception of the job: 'You're right. But we haven't identified the office in that way just yet. It will be up to you to do so, really. If you can.'

'If I can?' She thought he knew she could. She thought he knew her, accepted her own confidence. Now she realized that even if he did know, she would have to help him to prove it to his seniors. Yet he was not very far from the top of the organization; he had their trust as well as hers.

'I thought you knew what I could do, am doing, here, Dan,' she said, deciding to be firm about her own competence. 'I think my decisions so far have been more than just accurate; if Peter will work to me, rather than answering independently to you, you're right, we can build something very important here. If I get that authority, if you can promise that to me then I can deliver what you want.'

She grew animated with conviction, with that kind of professional energy which infused her happiest working life. He recognized it, enjoyed it, although he did not really think it necessary to success.

'No – you must have enthusiasm. It's like a light showing the way, or a force, an impulsion, I must have it, I couldn't enjoy life without enjoying work.'

Smiling at her over a pint, he was not envious.

'You're really hungry, aren't you, Louise? You really want this.'

The days when she thought it important to match men pint for pint were gone, she tasted her white wine and admitted that she was, although she hoped it didn't show. He was more amused by it than anything.

'It's a very young thing about you, the way you still

go after things you want. I used to think you were just aggressive, but that's not it, not really.'

'Not really.' At dinner she reminded him of his own admission, his own determination on a particular intent.

'That's not hunger, though. That's knowing where I fit, where I will fit. Hunger implies a lack of discrimination – for example, you're still searching. I've found what I want, all I have to do is chart my path to it.'

'And you've begun.' Something in the way she said this made it sound like approbation. They warmed to one another in a mutual assessment, and when he suggested that as he had never inspected the company flat this might be a good time to do so she reacted with pleasure although not, by then, surprise.

Outside her door he kissed her, his tongue running expertly between lip and gum.

'Oh, don't do that to me, Dan,' she moaned. 'I can feel the old sap rising.' And he laughed immoderately, thinking she had been funnier than she meant.

He touched with his finger-tip a yellowing bruise on her shoulder.

'I was a bit slow in mounting the other day; the animal bit me, just there, where I was leaning towards his head. My own fault.'

'Your own fault,' he murmured, his teeth edging lightly across the discoloured bone. He took possession of her quickly with his hands and mouth, but left her with nothing to do for him. She stroked his pleated ribs and searched beyond to touch, to press, but found her own hands stretching into a rigour which threatened to consume her.

He told her to be still and she obeyed instantly, shocked by some brutish instinct of response to this handling, but at last she could not be quiet and broke into a wrenching climax between his corded arms. She felt emptied, and tears bubbled up to fill the vacuum. He flicked a light, derisive kiss on her moist eyelids.

'You liked that.'

She could taste his smile as he moved away from her; her skin was grazed, she felt raw.

'I'm cold,' she said, shivering. 'Cover me.'

He warmed her then, through and through, and gently overcame her stiff resistant sobs until she acquiesced in his own pleasure and heard him sigh at last and slacken.

'You liked it, didn't you?'

She resented the question.

'Are you asking me, or telling me?'

'Both. I know it's true, and I want you to admit it.'

She did admit it: 'But it's the most selfish kind of making love I ever knew. I'm not sure I approve, really.'

He laughed out loud, and so at last did she.

'Louise. You must learn to be selfish then. Forget about approval – whose approval do you need, for this?'

His approval, perhaps. Or her own. Feeling as empty, as receptive as this, new ideas could float into her flickering consciousness, dousing the little wick of shame.

In the weeks, the months, that followed, she noticed how her body became a map of her habit of living dangerously. Something had happened to her, she was taking more risks, as if released from the constraints of propriety. Out riding she galloped more often, jumped more daringly, fell and her skin purpled and broke. With him she allowed roughness, welcomed his imprint on her soft flesh, although always, at first, the thrill was of shrinking from him.

It was during this time that they met for no other purpose. Her long-distance calls to him were thick with her intent. They had no secret words to signal with. Their uninvested communications were so ordinary, and so regular, that the same words meant either more or less as they desired.

'Come down for that conference,' he instructed her. 'We can meet and talk over that weekend.'

'Yes,' she answered. 'And will we meet?'

Of course. They would meet, and then they would meet as well. It was fun.

She was inclined to be more careful on his home ground. She preferred that their relationship would not be known to his immediate colleagues; that after all was head office, and she had to protect not just her own status there, but his. She remained aware that his ambition was not tethered to that one location, but that the organization centred there was crucial to his sense of purpose. And yet, and yet, some wild impulse made her strain to challenge that challenging relationship.

'Don't ring me at home again,' he said coldly. 'Do you understand? Never.'

She had done it deliberately, knowing. It was her home town, after all. She wanted to make him aware of her acceptance there, of her right not to be a stranger there with anyone. And it was autumn, a season which made her feel assertive, fearless, un-furtive. Driving past his house in the country, knowing he was inside, she pictured him sweeping the curled leaves from the avenue into a bonfire for the leaping children, saw him as she had never seen him, in an old sweater and wellington boots, a slavering labrador dogging his heels. Her road took her to the neighbouring hills where she noisily trod a forest path, imagining him catching up with her, a touch on her shoulder, incandescent surprise and then, joy.

Oh, suddenly she had wished for that ordinary joy, the smell of washing powder from his gansey, the dull sound of garden mud being knocked from his boots before he went into the kitchen, the things she knew he did, for he told her about them casually, although they were not casual. On a clear round lake swans herded their mottled cygnets, and when she had looked emptily at them for a while, standing as though waiting for something to happen, she walked slowly on until the path turned to edge a great grey field, its furrows undulating over acres until the rocks grew.

She superimposed on this the image of herself on

horseback, reins taut and her legs pressed down and under the barrel of the animal to keep him to the curve of the field in a dancing canter fuelled by the secretive, whispering autumn air. And then, out of the bend, she would answer the horse's question and her fingers would touch *yes* to the reins and they would – they would.

She had her ordinary joys, after all. Her bliss. So had he. After that phone call, to punish her, and she had known he would punish her, he had driven them both at a speed she found terrifying along roads which were not good. He would not allow her to put on her seat belt. He was not drunk. When he called for her and opened the car door for her she had felt some kind of coarse thrill, a definable *frisson*. When he was angry, even when she was his victim, in his power, she felt a power over him. And yet that cold rage made his masculinity more vivid, and more mysterious. She could almost enjoy making him angry for the sake of that re-assertion of the maleness of him, so that it was only right that her weakness should meet his strength, and that, if she were the victim of someone else, his strength would rescue her. Was this perhaps what men and women were about? Was it why women could tolerate brute servility to certain husbands; even when the male abuse was turned against them, they felt somehow reassured that it would be turned against anyone else who threatened them?

In the car, cowering from the throttled power that spun the steering-wheel on a fingertip, she sucked back her own fear. She could not look at the road that bucketed under them, she felt the bends as a force that flung her against the door to the scream of the tyres plunging over rough surfaces.

They had covered thirty vicious miles before he saw that she was crying, and another ten before he drew up so suddenly that she was jolted forward and hit her forehead against the polished dashboard. Her fright turned to anger. He sat away from her, not offering

136

comfort. At a button touch his window slithered down and cold air surged into the car. Inflamed by pain she stretched across and hit him hard on the face, her hand bunching automatically to turn the slap into a blow and she had the satisfaction of knowing that for once she had really, physically hurt him.

His head rocked back. Afterwards she was to remember how his hair trembled. But he began to laugh against the shock, and mocked her with his amusement.

'You're a dangerous woman,' he said lightly, his eyes glinting. 'I think we'd better go back. Put your strap on – and don't worry, I'll go easy.'

He drove carefully, they did not speak, but when she took her room key at the hotel he followed her along the white corridors and once inside the room he caught her and held her against him. She was not ready, and protested, pulling back until he bridled her face with his hands, his thumbs under her jaw and fingers spread to her hair. He kissed her so gently, with such tenderness, that her soul responded, and it became the act between them which seared itself into her consciousness of all life, all possibility, all love.

It was not then, but it did happen, that he called her his love. It happened on a visit south necessary for an unheralded reconnoitring of attitudes, possible decisions, bar-counter suggestions and plans about the future of the magazine. It was a time overlaid for her by loss of a story, a surrender she suspected to parochial pressures, or an unwillingness to recognize the fact that a meeting in Europe could transform requirements throughout the country.

She had been too circumspect, she felt, at the board meeting; the directors had to be persuaded gently, and she did not have the editorial reassurance she needed to convince them.

'Why did that happen, Dan?' She was sore in her defeat, felt humiliated. 'Don't they know we can't be afraid of the big time any more? Once we moved into Dublin we took on the whole bag – I thought they

137

understood that. It's not as if we're overspending, and Brussels wouldn't have cost us much anyway. Peter wanted to go, and he had all the contacts there lined up for interviews. We had the pics we needed on file, a lot of immediate stuff. It would have given us something really worthwhile to sell in the next issue – had you really tried to persuade them?'

She was going over all the arguments again. She couldn't let it go, she was shaking the whole débâcle like an old handbag to see what would fall out, looking for reasons beyond fear or obduracy. She walked up and down in his office, a new uneasiness clouding the anger at missing a story which everyone else was going to have, but she could have had first.

With one foot he pushed his chair back from the calm desk.

'Are you sure Peter wanted to go?'

She had been standing at the window, not seeing that well-known view of the long wide street fading into the scaffolded docks. His words warned her, she had already been given little hints, tilts, as she thought, at her confidence that the Dublin office was working well.

'He set the whole thing up. We planned it together, and then I left it to him, he only had to check back with me when he thought necessary. Of course he wanted to go – you know he loves that kind of political stuff anyway. And his name on the cover? Of course he wanted to do it.'

'What he didn't check back with you, then, was that he met our editorial manager on the train last week, and told him all about it. Don't misunderstand, Peter was enthusiastic, although I gather by the end of the conversation, as I heard it , his ardour had cooled a little. I think he was told to hold back for a few days. And I think, and you may as well face up to this, that the impression brought back to the editorial conference here was that you were moving too fast, too soon.'

After a silence she said: 'I can face that. All I have to do to face that is to tell Peter to button his lip. I can deal

138

with editorial cold feet; it's a pity that in this case an accidental meeting spoiled my strategy, but if that's all it was—'

He had to say it. 'It wasn't all it was. They are frightened by some of your proposals.'

'And?'

'Perhaps they have reason to be.'

She looked down towards the river where a ship lay open to the sunlight with all its limbs aslant.

'Do they know about us? Any of them?'

'No – I don't think so, I'm certain of that.' But he was surprised.

'If they don't know, and if you have nothing to hide from them apart from that, why haven't you told them how wrong they are? What have you been doing, Dan?' – *For me* was implicit, was it? So perhaps he was right, they were right, in that her thrusting forward was less for the company than for herself.

He got up quickly, and came behind her where she stood, still looking down into the sunny, winter street, her words as distant as if they came from outside the glass.

'Dan, do you think I'm wrong to believe that the Dublin office is where the real, competitive future of this company lies? Where it has to be located? And if I'm wrong, why are you warning me?'

His voice came from behind her; if she turned she could touch him, she could smell that trenchant, papery aroma which surrounded everyone who worked in that office, so close to the printing works and piles of newsprint, an aroma which implied a fellowship of which she had been part so gladly for all her working life.

'If I'm warning you, it's only to say that while of course you're not wrong, you have to be prepared to travel more slowly. For a little while, yet. That's all I'm saying.'

'More slowly?' She turned towards him then and, facing him, moved away so that he followed her and she looked at his face full in the flooding light of the window.

'Now, Dan,' and she smiled at him, tender with derision, 'now Dan, that's not like you. More slowly, but until when?'

'Well. It's a bit early to say this, perhaps. Just between us, then. And we can talk about it again, tonight maybe – will you?'

She nodded, not taking her eyes from his face, and he continued: 'Until my own position is secure. I'm moving now, and the Board are behind me. The full editorial management are prepared to buy what I can sell them, and they recognize my commitment to the whole enterprise, not just to this office or that office, not just to this publication or that one. Once that is consolidated my office will be *the* office; officially Head Office may still be here, with the works and administrative departments, but editorial management will centre on one particular position, mine. Eventually.'

'So.' She was at the door. She wanted to leave, quickly. 'So it's important that I'm not seen to be rushing my fences. Isn't that it, Dan?'

Her voice was tight with hurt. 'Do you think that at some stage you will let me know what your plans are for the staff in Dublin? Or does Peter already know?'

'Louise.' He went to stop her. 'Louise, my love—' But she was gone.

It was night before she got back to her hotel, having walked the city, recapturing its streets and emptying her mind of everything except resolution. It was cold, but she walked with her head up, climbing the terraced hills until her perspective gave her back all the pygmy proportions of places that have to be left behind.

At the hotel he was waiting for her, publicly in the foyer, and publicly he took her arm and walked with her to the lift.

In the bedroom she fought him silently as he pulled the clothes off both of them. When they collided on the cushioned floor she saw his legs roll whitely across her body and thought of the gelding she had used for schooling exercises only a few days before. Without his saddle he had roughly ploughed at the litter of the *manège*

140

and she had loosened the leading rein so that he collapsed quietly onto his forelegs and rolled his whole body ecstatically in the dust. A beautifully dappled grey, his belly grew white to the sheath and tail, and the great divided legs threshed with enjoyment, never touching her where she stood with his leash in her hands. All that he was lay there flailing before her, the bunched haunches, the iron legs with their plumes of unexpected frivolity, the wide flat neck surging from the chest, and the crested mane from which the creature, as he rose, shook the adhering fibre. His animality was complete, unchallenged even on her tether, and she remembered too that it was the animality that she adored when she admitted to herself that she adored these creatures.

The animality was innocent; the beast was what it was, and her own most essential enjoyment came when she adapted herself to its measures and strides. For the horses too there was adaptation, but she had never dared to look at circus horses, or wholeheartedly enjoyed the demonstrations of wondrous schooling in *haute école*. Even the races damaged them for her, being too hysterical, the curb too strong. Although some feeling for the fox prevented her from hunting she knew that out there on the ploughland and flaring fields the animal was as free as it could be in its attachment to mankind, and when she rode cross-country, or went down winter fields with feed, and called horses and ponies to her bucket and smelt the piercing clods of webbed grass as they cantered through the dusk, and then smelt their curious kindnesses – both joy and grief came in together, but the joy was strongest, for whatever was to come, she had known, touched, been part of a world wilder, more certain, more beautiful than her own.

On these thoughts she surrendered to him, whatever was to come.

'Wait,' she said then. 'Wait, I must fix myself,' but when he entered her on his own impulse he touched the rim of the diaphragm.

'Take it out,' he said, 'I want to spear you.'

141

Shaking in the bathroom, she wiped the spermicidal slime from her fingers before she rejoined him, knowing how dangerous this was, this was the final threat to her being. It was, it had to be, the last risk she would take, and despite the heat to which she would now at last submit she knew coldly that it would suit him, for a while, if she were dependent on his allegiance.

Even as she felt, not without sadness, the hoof-beats of his passion fade away from her, she was thinking of the letters she would have to write the next day, the action she would have to take. She had at last awoken to the realization that like many another woman she had not been taken seriously; although they had slept together, they had never worked together, and to him the hard reality of her life as a working woman had no permanence or imperative to match his own. What a mistake for her to make, though. And for so long.

He had never recognized that as he had plans, and places to go, so had she, and by now they were the same plans and places. In outline if not in detail. By moving quickly and without a backward glance she gave a presentation to the Board of all that had been done in the new departments, a commitment on her part to stay with it for a few years more in return for greater freedom of editorial action. She called up those national names, from politics, the church, business and cultural and educational establishments, clothed them in personalities friendly to the firm, clarified the connections, the power-lines, the potential, and did it without frightening them. They would, they decided, leave well enough alone, for the time being. And the time being was all the time she wanted.

She was not so breathless from this success that she did not see what she had done to him. She could not tell him, quite, that she had known what it would mean for him before she did it.

'At least,' she said, 'I did it from where you could see me. You were making plans behind my back, even though it was a back you rode on.'

'Were we not friends?' he asked her. 'Did you not know that I would have looked after you?'

'Perhaps I didn't want to be looked after by you. Perhaps that's not the kind of person I am.'

He was bitter. 'I would not have betrayed our friendship. I would never have ignored your abilities, or injured you deliberately. That's what I can't get over – you've been so deliberate.'

'Dan, you are talking absolute *shit*. I don't know what kind of late-Victorian language you want to use to disguise what you were doing, but in my words you were quietly and carefully limiting my life. And the fact that you don't see that is what is really so terrifying to me, that's the thing that left me no choice. If you had seen, and treated me as a worthwhile rival, a competitor, then I could have fought openly, cleanly, there might be something left to us. But you never knew me at all.'

He was silent. It was the saddest of meetings, this hasty, heckling closeness in her car, quickly parked in a crowded street.

'There were things about you that I knew. Still do know. And I thought you believed in me, as a friend, that our friendship was the thing above all that drew us together.'

She sighed, too loudly. He let his anger through. 'With all your reading, you should know what E.M. Forster said about choosing between betraying one's country or betraying one's friends.'

'I do know what he said. The trouble is that if you betray your country you *do* betray your friends, there's no way out of that. And don't attack me with literature; if betrayal comes into it the fact is that we both are guilty – you did it first, but I did it best .'

'Are you sorry, Louise?'

'Do you mean – will I miss you? Yes. I'm sorry.'

She was, too. Her success reduced the excitement of her life, and on the train, this train now going back to her office, she knew that one of her first actions would be to take down from the wall the reproduction of the

Géricault stallion. Would she lose all the rest? No, some resistant flare reminded her of what she would recapture when she went on horseback, and submitted to unalterably alien power, to strength beyond her own and independent of her, to a demand for an abandonment which she too desired but could not yet complete.

'But I did love him. I was so careful, but it was love, wasn't it? It must have been?' The question would last through these journeys yet to come, leaping to the light when the train entered this tunnel where on their one journey together he had kissed her so that the dark flamed with surprise. They were not finished with one another, she knew that. They were both young enough to know that the years stretched arms to include them; time and again, there would be time for reprisals.

In the hall of her small new house she saw the comforting dome of her riding-hat, the gleam of her boots; the appurtenances of her life, the typewriter, the answering-machine, the glossy objects which reinforced arrival, all proclaimed their faith in her continuance. Yet as she prepared tiredly for bed, stepping out of the bath she felt suddenly the flat, rubbery smack of her flesh, as if her body had a puncture.

At Home

Their frilled hair proclaimed them granddaughters. The children, perhaps, of the girl who had been adopted. Bernie's girl. A child herself at the time, Ellen had not understood, but had overheard words and pauses which illuminated, a light shining at an angle, a world beneath the cosiness of the sitting room where, one Thursday in every month, the aunts assembled.

Not one of them a blood relation – Delia, Molly, May and Bernie – and Ellen's own mother, Nell. They had been friends, hairdressers and typists together as young women. Only Bernie marrying above her station so that the others regarded her not as the interloper, but as the *ingénue* among them, the one who had to be shown how. Bernie was the only one who had not been a member of a tennis club, whose curls and smiles did not appear in the brown snap-album which chronicled their days of courtship, the picnics in Blarney and at Youghal, the women's puckered hair carrying with it even at this distance the viscous smell of perming lotion.

Surely these girls were granddaughters. Their faces sullen between wings of Pre-Raphaelite hair, they came nowhere near Bernie now where she lay in the glossy coffin, and stood instead together at the door of the funeral home, awkward and exquisite as they ignored the spurts of prayer around the decorated bier. How strange it was, considering that their mother had been adopted, that these two strange girls should have hair that matched so well with Bernie's own.

They never took their hats off when they came to tea, the aunts. Coats and gloves were taken upstairs to what the child's eye saw as the big bedroom, but the snug small hats stayed secure and tidy, full as cups of the familiar faces within. Only a hat could restrain Bernie's vigorous, shining whorls, richly black. No photograph had captured her as she stood with Nell in Patrick Street, the two young women suddenly turning their heads to look for – what, a voice, a child? The sun had come out then, catching the wheel of Nell's hat, fusing its silken lining into a translucence of rosy gold, burning the black of Bernie's curls into a pattern against her skin, the women transformed by light into an absence of being, of annulled motherliness, standing ablaze in the street before spinning apart again and becoming once more two friends in the sunlight, one of them her mother.

The granddaughters would have memories of Bernie, but none like that. By their time she crammed whatever she could find on her head, pulling it firmly down against the spring of the curls. The furious captured strands coiled against cheek and collar, softening all Bernie's impatient efforts to smartness as explained and exemplified by her friends.

Indeed, she was looking very neat now in the coffin. Tidiness had become even less important when her husband died, she had lost the picture of herself he carried with him. But now she lay here stiff with resented composure. The white hair was twisted into stillness, the hands obedient and quiet, there was no sprig of printed blossom to dance upon the high-necked un-ribboned nightgown. Only the wrinkled satin of her eyelids pretended at life, the lashes still dark, looking – it was only a trick of this moving candle-soft light – just for a second looking as if the dark brown sparkle must still glimmer beneath.

Alchemy only worked in retrospect. There was no magic here to transform the scene; memory was so random one could not be sure of what would survive from

146

this cluster of relatives and neighbours, their messages muted by the suave carpeting of the funeral reception rooms. There had been carpets in Bernie's home, or were they just remembered? What rituals those days had been, those once-a-month visitations. As Nell's daughter her memory's mystery composed itself around their own tiled hall and the rooms, since proved so small, on which the word genteel lay like a new, sad stain. Those were the days for the treasures of those days, the damask napkins, the ribbed china teapot, the cups and saucers traced with the faint purple of violets. The tiered cakestand. Ellen had never found out who had got the cakestand, afterwards.

Then it had soared from the linened occasional table, its plates skewered by the silver pole, its glories of pagodas and cherry blossom obscured by paper lace and the burden of thin pastry, wafers of sponge, light dressings of lemon curd or almonds, a delicacy called 'Maids of Honour'. Other plates offered crustless sandwiches oozing the cool green cucumber or the acrid, friendly tang of watercress from the stream in the glen.

The hands of the aunts had worked fluidly among skeins of wool; needles drew the shapes and colours of pansies embossed by embroidery silks. Nell introduced the adventure of crochet lace, its fragile intricacies a delight to their fingers.

As a child who should not have been there, allowed only because of winter-time ill-health, Ellen heard without understanding that little pitchers had big ears. She heard other things as well and did not understand them either – her own mother's late pregnancy, for example. She heard Nell announcing, in the impenetrable language sometimes used by adults, that she was expecting. The word fell into a total silence as the women, all of them in their forties, stared at Nell, who was not really smiling. Their eyes swivelled to the child sitting there – with one voice they chorused an order for fresh tea, for putting on the kettle.

Returning to the sitting room there was a new note in

147

the atmosphere. The constriction had gone and there was a flurry of voices all saying in one way or another the surprising word – 'Bernie!'

May's voice was heard most clearly, sharpest.

'I don't know when I heard anything so mad, Bernie. A child! Nell's bad enough – but yourself and Patrick! Sure how old are you, both of you?'

Nell hushed her, her tone bruised: 'Little pitchers.' There was no more to be heard that simmering afternoon. During the next months spare words of talk floated through half-closed doors, or dangled between grown-ups in the bus, or as they walked home from Mass. To be adopted was to be taken in, like an orphan in a book although you were not an orphan. And you could be too old to get children with your husband, so you could adopt a baby. Bernie was too old – or perhaps they had never tried. Perhaps, Ellen's boisterous father suggested slyly, they had not known how to try, and Nell looked shocked but she was pretending because she smiled a little secret look at him.

After those months there was a day when another child was present at Nell's afternoon. Not a baby: a girl of about eight years old, wearing pink pleated wool, with pink socks and shining black shoes with straps and a buckle low down at the side. This was Bernie's Ruth. Bernie seemed to think she was not there at all, only when the child sat down close to her she touched the light glossy curls, tucking them into order behind the pink ribbons. The talk was all mystery, and there was a litany of Bernie's voice saying – 'so Pat said' and 'Pat decided', and then sentences which all began with the word, 'finally'. No one else seemed to be saying very much. Molly ate steadily, pausing only to light a Sweet Afton which she smoked to the iridescent core and then thrust to smelly black dust in the crystal bowl at her side. Nell was fattening: her legs had thickened and she moved more slowly, allowing the graceful Delia to lift the plates, the teapot. May's mouth was tight, as if she would only talk in capital letters if she opened it.

Bernie's vibrant voice was sounding all the time, its rough, rusty notes explaining to them, pleading with them. Even when the children were outside the room, sent to play with one another, they could hear her, sounding happy.

There was no more Ruth for a long time after that. Nell's baby was born, there was the beginning of her first illness, the first breath of fear in the house, so empty when their father walked them back from the nursing home on Summer Hill. And here was Ruth now, alone in her seat next to the coffin. It was hard to remember when she had been seen, or where, after that first time. There had been talk, hadn't there, of a school none of the other aunts could afford for their springing families? There was a derisive key struck in a comment about 'one chick in the nest'. Ruth had been brought to a wedding, to the consternation of the adults, or maybe only of the aunts, and there she had been encouraged to sing, which she had done poorly in spite of her taffeta dress.

Nothing else was poor about Ruth. Yet among the aunts, when Bernie was not there, 'poor Ruth' became a phrase. There were things to report, a letter from a school: across the fragile china the words became longer, more difficult to remember. Illegitimate was one to be looked up in the dictionary, it meant something not known. There was mention of Dublin, and a boarding school, and May's crisp comment about 'more money than sense'.

Here was May now, arms and legs like twigs emerging from the bole of her fur coat. She leaned one shuddering hand on a walking stick as she made the sign of the cross, her fingers whispering against the filaments of fur, her face softly shielded by her folded hat. Her husband was with her, spry, the only mate to last as long as the aunts themselves. He went up to Ruth, taking her hand gently, and she knew who he was and spoke to him. He went back to support May, but Ruth did not let herself be kissed, and did not smile, or

149

respond in any way that could be seen to May's thick and halting words, and the old woman turned away to sit down heavily on one of the parlour chairs.

The room was filling up. Although not warm the chill was lifting, the voices and stamping feet from outside brought in a lightness, a sense of gathering. The granddaughters stood by the door, watching the scene of which they were a part, not going near their mother to whom everyone went, and the strangers to them who were of their grandmother's world did not know them or solace them, although they were noticed and assessed.

Clad in black from head to shoe, her face a wrinkled white flower beneath a bell of velours, Delia came in flanked by a son and a daughter-in-law. At even the short distance across the carpet she looked so exactly as she used to look that there was something inappropriate about her presence here, where all was transformation. There was the distance of time: she did not seem to be properly respectful of it. She seemed to bring in with her not just the comfortable family acolytes but courtiers. The truth must be different, but she had always been the beautiful one, speaking of 'engagements', her reciprocal afternoons had been heralded by the printed words '*At Home*' engraved gracefully on a white card, and in the hall of her house, visited in rapture, shadows of flowers dappled the walls.

Here too she brought flowers. The daughter-in-law carried a white crystalline froth of freesia and tulips, closed and cold and shivering as the people who came in constantly now were shivering, shaking off the cold outside. With the artistry unique to funeral parlours more flowers were mounted on timber frames around the room, but their strident colours evaporated as Delia advanced, her blackness quenching the soft drip of conversation around her. She knelt at the coffin, a stiff manoeuvring of limbs, but rose again without help. Taking the flowers from the acolyte hands she fitted them gently against the burnished wall of the casket, where they shone.

She went to Ruth, making no gesture, saying only in a thin and distant voice which everyone heard, 'She was a wonderful woman. And a very good mother indeed.' There was no emphasis in her words, no hint of feeling, only of knowledge, as if that were enough.

Something stirred in Ruth's face. She turned into the embrace of a cousin from Dublin, first in what was now a queue of people waiting to give the formal condolence. Delia walked steadily back to her family group, by now a growing circle into which she fitted like a stem. She had stood like this at Nell's funeral, at Molly's too, a fulcrum while May revolved on the perimeter, all the children younger then, and Ruth not there.

Then she had been missing, wasn't that it, because her husband had left her? No catching up could be done now, but something had happened and tugged at the memory: something between the expulsion from boarding school and the end of her marriage about which Bernie had spoken in tearful whispers. It had yielded anyway these two girls. It seemed as if Ruth had never been a daughter herself: there had been the orphanage, then short-lived family life with Bernie and Patrick, then the school in Dublin, then marriage at what – seventeen? Could it have been so young? She did not look much older now, but her years since then had been chronicled among the tea-cups, italicized words in the arena of the small, diminishing sitting room.

That was it, the words came back, no need by then to look at the dictionary. Ruth had had a daughter before she married, and then the other girl was born, and then the marriage over, its purpose served. Ruth stayed in Dublin, but the babies were sent down to Bernie, and she had brought them to Nell's funeral a few years later. They had been shining with health, identical in blue coats, one tall and thin, the other round and merry-faced, not alike. Different fathers, perhaps. May had wondered.

They looked more similar now, spare and contained as Ruth herself, no flicker of emotion between the

151

curtains of hair. Surely this was a kind of homecoming for them? Ellen remembered some rhythm to their appearances and disappearances at Bernie's pretty little bungalow, but she had not paid much attention to what she had heard about them, or seen. There was so much she had not understood, nor wanted to understand. In this crowded room now, a tender young priest spoke slowly, as loving in the banal words as if he had known Bernie. The commonplace ritual wove itself around the company, she saw the faces which had emerged while she was not looking, sons and daughters of parents known to her and now dead, no one who recognized her.

It was for Bernie she was here, anyway. The discreet curtain was drawn before the coffin by the sleek executive undertaker, and she saw how Bernie's hand had reached for the curtain-rail that day in the hospital, pulling the blossoming cotton around Nell, who lay helpless against the pillows while Bernie sobbed.

'It's not for myself,' Bernie had turned from Nell to explain her grief. 'I love having them, they're lovely little girls. But Ruth: I just don't know what she's doing, and she won't allow me to help in any way at all.'

'But you are helping, Bernie, giving the children a safe place to stay – that's helping in a very important way.'

Nell's voice was light, but the words were weighted with consolation.

'You've always done your best for Ruth. If things went wrong you can't blame yourself, or Patrick. Perhaps it all began before you even saw Ruth. Perhaps—'

Bernie knew what was meant.

'I know. I know all that. We took her too late, we should have taken a baby. I wanted to. I *did* want to. But Nell – I was afraid of what you all would say, that it would all seem ridiculous, me with a new baby. Can you imagine, May? She knew I was older than the rest of you.'

'Not so much older, Bernie. After all, we were still having children – I was, remember?'

152

They remembered together, smiling.

Molly had been there too, that day in the hospital. Breathless with children, she remained the only one of the aunts who had not caught up with their expectations.

'For God's sake, Bernie, don't be going on like that. You had a chance to get a child without going through the first few years and you were right to take it. There's a time in your life when you're able for small children, and a time when you're not, and you did the right thing.'

She was not allowed to smoke in the room and sat uneasily beside the bed, twisting her hands in the strap of her handbag. All her grief had been for Nell. To Bernie she was brusque, rallying, things could be so much worse.

'It was just that we thought, you know, we thought if we took her at about five or six she'd be over the difficult stage.'

'Ah, Bernie,' said Nell, looking fondly beyond Molly, 'they're never over the difficult stage, never as long as we live.'

'And Ruth says – Ruth says she doesn't want to tell me what's happening because I get too upset about it. But Nell, why shouldn't I get upset? Someone *has* to get upset about things that go wrong.'

She was right, Nell said, her own voice fading, tired; there was no energy left to fight with for Ruth, even for Bernie.

'You're right, Bernie.' Her words came slowly. Things were beginning to drift away from her.

'You're right. Those little girls, they're entitled to your indignation. They're entitled to know that what's happening to them is not right, that it makes you angry. That someone is angry for their sake. Even if you can do nothing else.'

It was coming to nothing else, nothing more, for all three of them. Nell died at home. After all in her own bedroom, helped from the world by the children she had

153

brought into it, held by the husband who had lain down with her in bed the very night before. Her Bavarian china cups had sparkled in the careful hands of friends, and the house was full of the cumbersome smell of great globed chrysanthemums. A single white rose had been placed between Nell's stiff fingers where it bloomed among the Rosary Beads.

May had been there, animated by friends from long ago, from the photograph albums. Molly had offered her slackening cheek to the kisses of women and of women's husbands who might some time, some day, have tried to help her. Delia was there, impassive, and Bernie's rich voice was roughened with talk as she went from sitting room to kitchen, showing the little girls how china should be washed, how the doilied plates of sandwiches should be handed around. It was Bernie who found, and put away without a word, the half-made crochet place-mat, its hook still linking the unfinished web.

After Nell's death Molly had succumbed to widowhood, neglecting herself into tuberculosis and too late to a state sanatorium, dying comfortless, untidily, her washing done by Bernie and May, May and Delia paying for the funeral, quietly damping down the sniffed sorrows of that large family.

They had all lived in the same parish, the aunts, sharing the same church. It was the sanctuary of their lives. Nell, and then Molly, had died to the last murmurs of Latin. For Bernie now the priest waited at the door, the light coming from behind where the neighbours stood inside from the dark and cold while the hissing cars drew up to the familiar steps. In this darkness one of the granddaughters stumbled, reaching out quickly to clutch one arm among the many outstretched to help her. Her mother was not near, although they had come to the church in the same car. The girls had kept their distance, close only to one another. Now the one who had nearly fallen recovered, shook back her hair, and her sister lifted from the steps a tumbled bunch of flowers, more petals falling from the loose binding as she winnowed them free of dust.

But they must remember this church. Bernie had brought them to it, they had been to a school only a hundred yards along the road. Yet who could tell what would be remembered of what was happening, when it was happening? They entered now as strangers and did not join their mother who sat in the front pew, next to the bier and the piled contortions of the floral tributes. Alone, and moved slightly apart from the coloured mass lay Delia's offering, like a flat flame. The two young girls walked together down the aisle in a silence which had not been meant for them but which they interrupted, there was something purposeful about their advance.

At the coffin, at the altar, they neither knelt nor blessed themselves. Their veiled faces had nothing to say to the priest who stood arrested in a gesture of welcome. One of them touched the coffin, lightly. The other put on it the decomposing spray, winter jasmine, winter iris, the lenten rose, white and purple heather, the smokey greenness of eucalyptus leaves which, bruised by their fall, let out an odour reminiscent of old, familiar remedies.

What garden had they plundered for these trophies of the habitual, the commonplace? The familiar. What children were they, then, to make this statement, to assert a selfhood separate from all that might have been expected of them? Their trenchant gesture broke through the conventions of the funeral. The woman who was spending her last night on earth in this echoing church had never been called Bernie by them, Bernie was their unknown. The coffin would wait through the night beneath the sky-blue ceiling, and on it would rest the broken spray, the scarred and cautious flowers of the cold.

No one tidied them away. After Mass next morning the priest shook the blessed water on them, and they could be seen to tremble on the coffin when it was

155

trundled, there being no men of the family to carry it, out through the door to the hearse waiting by the steps. The two girls were there again, but walked with Ruth as the passing bell was rung and strangers on the street outside crossed themselves. There were fewer people at the church than at the funeral home, and fewer still journeyed on to the graveyard. The cold, they told one another as the hard sun shone down on them. Nothing for it but to stay inside, this weather.

This time the granddaughters walked immediately after the coffin: they held hands. Ruth and other relatives stood in a small embankment of formal mourning as the coffin slithered down the ropes. The green plastic rug was placed euphemistically across the hole, and on this the bright flowers were piled, the sheafs and sprays and wreaths, not so many that Delia's delicate blossoms might fade in contrast, but in contrast seemed full of light and sweetness. Beneath, in the dark, the garden flowers had been buried.

Delia was there, with another son, another daughter-in-law. May had gone home after the Mass: her husband had called her 'old girl' and warned her against the wind. Delia stood at the edge of the grave and looked steadily into it, and did not join in the responses when the priest recited the Rosary, only the first decade, the first glorious mystery. She was not quick to move away, although she did not speak to Ruth or to any of those remaining. Her son looked stalwart, tweedy and resilient, and spoke with smiles to those around him, making sure that everybody had a lift, asking who was going to the Fox and Hounds for a warmer, he would join them there after. *After* would be after Delia and his own wife had been brought home, and now he ushered them carefully towards the wicket gate and the cars.

There by the wicket the two young girls loitered, as if they did not know where to go next. In the last strolling group their mother moved towards them. Despite the sneaking wind there was something reluctant in her step as she left Bernie behind. Slowly she walked up to her daughters. Together they walked out under the great trees around the gate.

Ellen watched them crouch to enter the waiting car. The cold touched her. Looking up she saw how the wind suddenly savaged the trees, and how the startled birds flew up crying and scattered through the air, like seeds.

Divorce Papers

'Where are my divorce papers?'

Mona's voice sent the children scattering among the rooms.

'I had them all there together under the telephone! Somebody moved them! I've got to have them now – come on! Where are they?'

She strode shrieking through the house. Homework copies were lifted, thrown down again. Books were shoved aside – *Méthode Orange*, Longman's Latin Grammar, *Peig*, Ed McBain.

'Who's reading Ed McBain?'

The cover showed a hypodermic needle and a feather. Drugs and birds.

The eldest, fifteen, claimed the paperback without shame.

'It's only the usual, Mum. You know: *Winter held the city in its grip. Patrolman Delanty would have sworn if his breath hadn't frozen* – that kind of thing. *You* know.'

She knew, having enjoyed all the seasons of the 87th Precinct. She supposed she couldn't complain. It wasn't exactly *The Old Man and the Sea*, but reading was reading and he was probably too old, at fifteen, to accept her censorship. He was old enough for responsibility:

'Did *you* see my divorce papers? In a brown folder? Did you take the folder?'

She had a dim memory of an urgent request for school stationery the previous week.

'*Did* you *take* the *folder?*'

His look told her that her tone of the moment was the

precise reason why he had not done any such thing.

The telephone rang: could she leave immediately, and collect two trays from Eileen on the way down, they would expect her at ten-thirty at the latest, they had to be well ready before Mass began at eleven. She was not to forget the plastic bags, small ones would be best, and if she had any of those freezer trays she might as well bring them. And freezer tags. And a couple of biros. Eileen wasn't able to go after all, so there would be only herself, Phyllis, Goretti—

'Nance!' Mona didn't mean to sound too sharp, but really if there was a rush on what was the point of staying talking like this?

The point was—the trouble was Bill had changed his shift roster, and now Nance had to make up a curry to leave him for lunch, and she hoped he'd be able to manage—

Thinking of Nance's curries Mona hoped he'd remember to put salt in it.

'It's all right, Nance. I'll leave now and I'm bringing a good deal of stuff of my own. I'll collect whatever Eileen has ready, and I'll be there in twenty minutes. Don't worry!'

She slapped down the phone and turned to find her daughter carrying a box of cakes to the car. In the kitchen her son was carefully lifting the bags of meringues into another box, where they sat upon sugared sponges and long loaves dark with fruit.

'Come on, Mum' – her daughter held up the smarter of the two jackets she possessed. Pushing herself into it she was told not to worry, they would look for the papers while she was out, once she was sure, was she? that they were not in the office?

She was sure, and ran.

Without lipstick, as she discovered when she got back into the car outside Eileen's contorted gate.

So that's why she looked at me as if I was a poor relation, Mona thought, reaching into her handbag for the Lancôme Christmas present – thank God for

159

sisters! – just the right shade of rose and soft enough to make the two painted peaks in the middle of her upper lip look what the carton said would be 'charmingly natural'. The coloured salve made a big difference, even to the way she felt about herself, and she drove the packed car undeniably lighter of heart.

Always it happened down here, anyway, a lift of the spirits in this five-mile tunnel of trees which led away from the city to the south. The day was crisp with the business of autumn, and from the sleek gardens reaching the road there came the tang of bonfires, so woody and natural that it was almost surprising to remember that it belonged to the coiffured lawns beyond the trees. When they were passed and the smell remained Mona remembered too that she had not had a bath after her own bonfire the night before.

Saturday was a great night for a garden fire, especially when some gardening had been done and there were twigs and prunings and woody bits and pieces for the burning. The children still relished the crunchy piles of leaves heaped in the lane and along the garden path, and they teased the cats which crouched in the trees so that they could be curious in safety. And there were all those newspaper headlines to be read before they shrivelled forever in one last blaze, the flames gusted upwards after rake and hoe had let in the air. Children came from gardens away down the road to take it in turns to race the wheelbarrow up the composted stack of weeds and earth and shake it empty onto the hungry sparks beneath. And then the wind would blow the smoke the wrong way and even the most stalwart would howl and hop with the smart until they retreated all together to the kitchen where they would not put on the light but watch from the dark the soaring and crumbling of the distant flames.

It was a ritual, a heightened sense of being at one with their world; when the smells came from other fires up and down the road, or even from the cautious leaf-burning from the immaculate garden next door, there

160

was even a sense of holiness, something time and custom had established as essential to well-being.

Smiling to herself at the goodness of it all, it was enough, it was enough, Mona began to sing and found she was warbling an old hymn. Indeed, there was a Church Chapel or Meeting look to the occupants of the cars that thumped past her – going in to the sung Mass at St Mary's, perhaps, now the only possessor of the Victorian gothic graces which had once distinguished the city churches. Mosaic and polished timber were being replaced or covered with ropy red carpet. Crenellated altars had been thrown out, the baize-lined collection plates had given way to plastic basins of the kind used as drinking bowls for dogs. Altar-cloths, those miracles of damask and lace, had vanished, possibly eventually rubber mats would take their place, as rubber plants had been deemed an acceptable decoration where the vulgarity of blossom offended some important eye. All that brass, of candlestick and tabernacle and thurifer, so thin and bright it might have been gold, all that was gone and with it the glitter and shine and invitation which illuminated the profession of faith.

She thought of Talleyrand – 'Above all, gentlemen, no zeal.' Right enough, decorative enthusiasm had been banished, churches were as smooth and undemonstrative as offices, streamlined out of their mystic existence. John XXIII probably felt it was quite safe to leave revision of the liturgy in the hands of the Italian hierarchy; what he knew nothing about was the effect of cultural famine on the Irish clergy – always embattled, always afraid, always ignorant and never curious. Give them responsibility for words and music and you might as well start preaching from the *Beano*.

Her voice, happy in the enclosure of the car, rose again:

Hail Queen of Heaven,
The Ocean Star,
Guide of the Wanderer here below,

161

Thrown on life's surge,
We claim thine aid,
Save us from peril and from woe.
Mother of Christ,
Star of the Sea,
Pray for the Wanderer,
Pray for me.

Follow that, she thought, mentally addressing the proponents of the 'clap your hands for Jesus' school of church hymnals.

O gentle, chaste,
And spotless maid,
We sinners make our claim to thee –
Remind thy Son
That He has paid
The price of our iniquity.
Mother of Christ,
Star of the Sea,
Prayer for the sinner,
Pray for me.

But Mona had to admit that she herself used religion like a spectator sport. Even in the matter of the divorce papers she had taken a stand somewhere outside the pale of the Church, the Big C as she was now inclined to call it, more or less deliberately.

She accelerated: the others would have their smiles sharpened waiting for her – and she might have to leave them early too, they all forgot that she had to work for her living, even at weekends. A Renault, a Ford Sierra and a Datsun of the larger kind were shining in the little forecourt as she turned her travel-scarred Mini into the space beside the sacristy. The church was small, grey and simple, but it had a steeple, and a real bell which rang not just for Mass and the Angelus but at the old prescribed monastic hours of matins and prime and compline, sounding gently among the small wooded hills of this countryside.

Inside, where the Italian tiles were dulled by the shoe-leather of an earlier congregation, the husband of the Renault, big and smooth like the car, was affably prepared to give her a hand with getting what he called the goodies out of the car. Mona knew all about the kind of hand he could give and what he really meant by goodies but she smiled anyway and told him the boot was open and she'd be delighted if he could bring in everything for her.

She no longer believed in refusing gratuitous offers of help – life was too hard and too short. And there was an element of mischief in her dealings with Danno – she accepted his hints and doubled them and like most men he was frightened out of his wits. Now he came panting with bravura up the steps, and Phyllis, polished from dark curls to bright toes, exclaimed in distress and went to help him. 'My old Duck,' she called him, and he grinned savagely.

A long trestle table had been donated by the monks for whose indirect benefit this cake sale was being held, and on this Phyllis and Nance had laid the trays of cakes, the latticed apple tarts, the thick chocolate circles stuffed with fudge, their black icing studded with violets. Scones fresh with a smell to melt butter in a fridge were piled on plates, and there were plates too of biscuits, shortbread, brownies rich with oatmeal and golden syrup. Everything shone under a frost of cellophane, and Mona's unpacking caused a brief rearrangement so that Eileen's pizzas and quiches, luscious with cheese and tomatoes and peppers, had a sign of their own: 'Savouries.'

Nance was counting the cash float, and Phyllis looking round quickly to make sure there were no unwelcome listeners, continued the story interrupted by Mona's arrival.

'She said that he told her that Rachel had taken everything, right down to the cutlery: "My own mother's knives," he said to her, and she said it would bring the tears to your eyes thinking of him there in that huge

163

house with the children at boarding school and Rachel taking everything, even his own mother's knives!'

Nance's mouth was an avid scarlet oval, but before she could hear any more Goretti arrived, laughing and apologetic, with Con, carrying the laden plastic bags. Round-faced and plump, Goretti was ageing obviously and cheerfully, 'greying at the edges', as she said herself.

'God! Isn't this gorgeous!' – she surveyed not just the fragrant, glittering board, but the tubs of chrysanthemums flanking the inner doors to the church, the mahogany lustre of pews and confessionals, the glazed white whorls on the altar reflecting the gladioli and exuberant begonias along its ledges, leaving in stark contrast the bare wooden plinth before it. Opening the doors Goretti released the fragrance of gardens and, kneeling, she blessed herself quickly, bowing her head for a silent minute before rejoining the others in the hall.

'That reminds me,' said Nance, 'I'll leave you at Communion for a few moments, I haven't received all week,' and Goretti, shaking herself, Mona thought, free of her instinct for devotion, said that really, she had doubts about these ecclesiastical cake-sales.

'I mean,' she said, 'I was just saying to Con on the way down, when you see it all set up here like this, you'd nearly expect Jesus to come along with a whip to drive the money-changers out of the temple!'

'Ah, it was the money-*lenders* he threw out, Retta' – Con enjoyed teasing her still; he never let her forget that her Christian name invoked a questionable saint. 'I'd say he'd allow a bit of this kind of thing all right – especially if he tasted any of it!'

'All I know,' said Nance, who felt vaguely uneasy with these marital amiabilities, 'is that I never want to bake another cake, pie, or biscuit; it's all right for some—' she looked quickly at Phyllis'—who can just take the stuff out of the deep-freeze. The rest of us have to work our fingers to the bone for this affair, you know.'

She had a sensitive notion of grievance, Nance. It was aggravated now because Phyllis, in response to Goretti's inquiries about the new house, was explaining how she had just that weekend completed redesigning the basement in Tudor. Con and Danno had gone out for a cigarette, and Phyllis was in full flow.

'The house had to be gutted, of course, before we could *touch* it.' She turned to explain to the others:

'You know those old houses, it's a half-timbered Georgian, of course you won't find many of them about, and then the builders try to blind you with knowledge, but as Danno said, if we didn't go to school at least we met the scholars on the way back so we insisted on our own plans being carried through. Danno knew a very good draughtsman, so he was very firm about it. "It's our money, and our house, Phyllis," he said to me, and honestly, it's the only attitude to have, isn't it?'

Mona's eyes met Goretti's for a brilliant second, and they agreed, oh yes, it was the only attitude to have. Nance couldn't bear it, and pitched in with a careful query about Phyllis' cousin, the Malone girl – that marriage?

'Oh, it was lovely!' Phyllis didn't quite know what Nance was after: 'Jill looked wonderful, absolutely wonderful—'

'In white, I suppose?' Nance declared herself.

Phyllis could afford to be dignified, to ignore the suggestion: '*No*, actually. It was a cream silk from Ib Jorgenson, with orchids, and a coronet of matching flowers. And the reception! At their home, of course – in the gardens, it was just wonderful.'

'God, I don't know.' Goretti moved in to separate them. 'I'd want a three-year guarantee now before I'd give anyone a wedding present. Still, I'm delighted for Jill, she's a lovely girl. But, Phyllis, how's her mother? How's Cora?'

The decorated edges of Phyllis' eyes showed suddenly pink. Mona could have asked too, but would not, for fear.

'Oh, she's fine now. She had to go in after the wedding.'

She stopped to gather the words.

'They took the other breast off. And she has to go through all the rest of it, injections, wigs, the lot. Still, she's very cheerful, really.'

Nance, her voice stifled, asked what Mona was thinking, what they were all thinking:

'There's three left at home now, aren't there? How old is the youngest?'

He was six.

The women looked at one another. Mona's own face was blank, but she could feel what passed between them all, the scraping of bone on bone beneath the skin. Crepitation. They shared the hint of doom, the treason of their own bodies. For Mona there was this extra: a mother on her own, she had long ago realized that nothing more terrible could happen to her children than that something should happen to her. As she aged, as they aged, she counted each day towards a completion and a release from the tension of this fear.

The time had nearly come, now. So far she had got them to their middle teens. Not only that: only yesterday, before the bonfire, she had overheard them:

'What's the terrible mess in the backyard about?'

'It's all right, it's only Mammy gardening.'

There was something truly reassuring about that exchange, it marked their arrival at a distance from her.

The men came back, an advance party. People were coming, and a sandalled priest opened the doors, nodding to them but not speaking, already caught up in the silence and sense of the mystery he was to celebrate.

The sale of the cakes began, with children as spies and embassies essential to successful sales. Mona had already selected for herself the job of wrapping, but still found traces of cream or jam or chocolate sticking to her fingers as she worked. A small boy and a smaller boy – seven perhaps, and six – handed up a grubby pound note and pointed in turn to the items they

166

wanted to make up their dozen 'fancies'. A young woman in a tightly-belted coat, her hair drifting from under a dull headscarf, waited for them until finally she said she would wait inside or there wouldn't be anywhere to sit. Mona parcelled their eventual purchase as neatly as she could, handing them over with a smile, but the boys were impassive and vanished limply into the crowded church.

The hallway was heavily quiet when the doors were closed once again. The priest was on the altar, there was the sturdy surge of sound as the responses were set into rhythm. Silver was piled into pounds on Nance's cardboard plate, and Mona saw with satisfaction that all the meringues were gone. Phyllis and Goretti re-arranged what was left – not a lot, thank heavens, said Con, and Danno went off to drop in at the golf-club.

Phyllis noticed, and said to Nance that she'd go to Communion with her; Nance looked towards Mona and grimaced, lifting eyes and eyebrows.

'Say one for me!' Goretti whispered as Phyllis wiped her hands and blotted the lipstick on her mouth.

'I always hate to receive with lipstick on,' she confided in return. 'And I could never imagine myself taking it in my hands – it takes all the respect out of it, doesn't it? Still, I suppose they know what they're doing ...' Her voice faded on a hint of doubt, and she followed Nance into the monastery corridor from where they could slip through a side door into the church.

'Poor Phil,' was all Goretti said; Con said they would give her a lift home, but Goretti laughed and thought it was unlikely that Phyllis would enjoy being shaken to bits in the old Toyota.

'Danno will call back for her. Probably,' she told Con, only so that they might wait and see.

Mona enjoyed being with Goretti and Con. They treated each other, even at their most casual, with the same cheerful kindness they showed to everyone. That their apparent stolidity hid a fruitful private relationship Mona knew from a rare hint dropped by Goretti:

167

'he's as hectic as the next fellow' was the comment when Mona once wistfully noted Con's undemanding amiability. They both choked and laughed with the surprise, Goretti pink with merriment.

'Oh,' she gasped at last. 'Oh, don't ever let men fool you that way, they're always up to something!' And she looked at her thin hell-raiser with eyes brimming with jovial relish.

Now that she thought of it, Mona realized that Goretti reminded her of Mrs Barriscale, a much-married widow of her childhood terrace. An upright, handsome woman with a house predictably full of children, she had an air of exotic interest because of her two widowings.

There was also the marvel of her Saturday clean-outs. Wet or fine, every Saturday throughout the year – in those days in the terrace no one ever went on holidays – she locked all the children out of the house at nine o'clock in the morning and they weren't let in again until six in the evening, when one by one they were marched up the stairs and into the re-filled bath. In the meantime they took refuge in various houses up and down the street, and at lunchtime Mrs Barriscale pushed their sandwiches out through the letter-box.

Mona had seen her most recently in a supermarket, perhaps two years ago. Still upright, still handsome, she pushed a loaded trolley before her as majestically as if it were one of those enormous, high-sided sprung prams in which she had reared her double brood.

She was shopping not for herself, but for Sandra. Poor Sandra.

Thinking quickly, Mona assessed Sandra as being about thirty now; was she ill?

No, thank God. *Working*.

Mrs Barriscale pronounced it carefully, as though it were a contagious disease. Sandra had two children, you see. And – she leaned closer and dropped her prominent voice – himself had left her. Well, actually, Sandra had thrown him out, and good riddance. Mrs

168

Barriscale had warned her, long before that marriage –
and wouldn't you think that Sandra would realize that
Mrs Barriscale knew what she was talking about? But
no, nothing would do Sandra but to marry him.

'Two children in two years, Mona! But at least she
managed to keep her job – or she did because I kept the
children for her. *He* was useless. Useless! Dancing in
the disco the night she was in hospital having her
second! Isn't it funny now, the way there'll always be
people who tell you that kind of thing . . . Still, it was a
kindness to Sandra in the end, and she threw him out. *I*
couldn't say a word, mind you – but at least she saw
sense in the end.'

Straightening herself from this unburdening, she
turned confidently to Mona and asked after her sisters,
her father, her own family, her husband.

Mona reported faithfully and fluently. Then she had
to say it: the husband was not living with them any
more. Oh, everything was fine, they were all grand
really but, well, yes, they had separated.

Mrs Barriscale leaned heavily on the bar of the
trolley.

'Well, my God, Mona, Well, *my* God.'

She turned away again, looking down the long
enticing aisles before her. Slowly she began to shake
her head.

'Do you know, Mona,' and she still looked away, 'do
you know what I say to myself? What I say to myself is,
at least it's decent when you bury them. Isn't that it?'

That was it, Mona thought now, an overheard invoca-
tion from the church reminding her of sudden funerals,
the decency of them, tear-sodden rituals which left
everything said, decently done with.

The church door swung open violently, pushed by the
woman, Mona recognized her, who had been waiting for
the two small boys and their cakes. She was only a girl,
or seemed so in her distress. She was shaking, her
hands tearing at the knot in her belt as though to tear
the coat open, to let herself breathe.

She was crying, her face bitter and red. Through the door she had left open came words Mona had been half-hearing but, having no relevance, had been meaningless. Now they rang clear.

'. . . true indissolubility, we must ask ourselves what it means. We must not be in doubt about the eternal nature of this bond, the bond sanctified by sacrament! Those sacred words confer the blessing on the bond which, let us say it again, and again for there are those who will not hear us, the bond which no man can break. *"Let no man put asunder!"* We can read that confidently today, my dear brethren, as saying – let no *legislation* put asunder, for who can interfere with the fundamental principles of our Holy Catholic Church?. . .'

A fistful of words, but the young woman moaned as they punched through the door. She crouched in the chair Goretti had pulled out for her.

'How can they? How can they?' – she gasped her words on sobs. Goretti was holding her, soothing her.

'Don't mind him, lovey, he's only saying what he's told to say, don't mind him at all . . .'

'But can't he see? I'm not the only one in the bloody church who's without her husband? Can't he see us, look at *us*?'

She had left her children inside. Now they came banging through the door, and even from the hall Mona and Goretti could register how their mother's groaning desperation met and splashed against the assured tones of the man at the lectern, one a fluid ululation, the other clean, firm, insoluble. Unconcerned now that they were within her sphere again, untouched so far by the passion of an anger they recognized but could not interpret, the boys used their parcel of cakes as a football up and down the glossy hall.

'How can he say such things?'

Goretti's platitudes had quietened the woman's voice. She rocked on the chair, Goretti's hand on her shoulder, Mona whispering, 'I know. I know.'

They all knew. How could he say such things? Here,

to women on their own, bringing their children to church, remembering confession and hair-cuts and the milk-money for school, battening down against the other surges of life in order to fasten just this one, the measured promise of normality, of acceptance within a given people.

'I'd divorce him in the morning. I would. I *would*. I'd divorce him in the morning if I could, no matter what they'd say. And I'd still go to Mass, *and* to Communion, and I wouldn't care, some things are just plain wrong and they've no right to pretend they don't know it. They've no *right!*'

Her pain gripped them in a fusion of anger, not just on her behalf.

'I had to get out of there. For the first time in my life I couldn't listen to a priest at Mass. What is happening to me? What will happen to me?'

Goretti tried to smile, to reassure her:

'Sure I never listen to them at all. I just sit there, letting it all roll off me. I wasn't a week married before I realized that they haven't a clue, God love them. You're not tough enough, that's all.'

'Not yet,' added Mona.

The young woman raised a face like a damp pink blossom to her.

'You'll get tough enough for anything,' Mona assured her. 'I've been through something of the same kind. I know what you're trying to do, keeping the children secure, denying your own wants, not asking for help. You're right to do all that, don't doubt it. Just – don't expect *them* to take any notice.'

'That's very hard,' the woman said slowly.

'Yes, but it does get easier, after a while. I promise you.'

Mona wanted to inject some of her own confidence into her, to help her become proud of defiance.

'You'll learn that it doesn't matter what they think or what they say. If what you have to do is right, then you have to do it without waiting for the approval of

171

anyone else. Approval is a kind of luxury, you know, we can live without it; once you're sure, yourself, then you have to go ahead.'

Into their small silence came the silver sound of the Consecration bell. The woman began to push her straying hair under her scarf, a tissue replaced the wad of kitchen paper Goretti had thrust into her hands.

The man's voice came through the door on an eruption of conviction:

'This *is* the Lamb of God who takes away the sins of the world, *happy* are those who are called to His supper . . .'

'I'll just go in to the back after this,' the woman said, fastening her coat. 'I always like to get the blessing. You'd miss Benediction, wouldn't you? I really do miss that, the feeling of being blessed.' There was a lost sound in her voice.

Goretti had put another plate of cakes together, and scribbled a list of telephone numbers, including her own.

'Take this, and use it any time you want to,' she said. 'We'll mind the cakes, and the boys, until you come out.'

The woman thrust the piece of paper into her pocket, accepted the parcel with a rueful smile, but took the children with her. Both Mona and Goretti knew she was feeling ashamed of herself; she did not want to talk to them afterwards, or to meet them.

'I suppose she won't ring any of those people on the list,' said Goretti with regret.

'No,' said Mona. 'She doesn't want to think she might be like me' – and Goretti did not answer.

Nance returned on a gust of talk.

'I hope I'm not uncharitable now, but really, this Minister of the Eucharist business! When I saw who was handing out the Host I just put up my hand in front of my mouth to show I would wait for the priest. Do you know who it was?'

She turned to Phyllis.

'Did you receive from Mrs Leahy? Remember her in the Primary School, the time she gave my Larry? She flaked him from one end of the class to the other – and I'm expected to receive Communion from her!'

Phyllis, looking around for Danno, said that no, she hadn't gone near Mrs Leahy. 'I'm not quite humble enough yet,' she smiled, gently ashamed of the little joke.

The final clearing up was quickly done, and Phyllis went home with Goretti and Con, asking Mona only if she saw Danno, if he came back having mistaken the time, to tell him where she had gone. 'Tell him I'm all right,' she said, reminding them all that he cared.

At her own door Mona was met with the surreptitious hiss of soup boiling over, the tender smell of chicken in the oven. A fire brimmed in the hearth, and the divorce papers had been found. The hours of the afternoon were profitably spent at work on what she liked to think would be the definitive article on the subject, the indexed teasing-out of links and contradictions, law canon and secular. 'No case histories,' she had agreed with the editor, it was too serious for that. Yet as she assessed her material again, before her impassioned fingers throbbed along the keys, she hesitated for a moment, thinking of that football of cakes.

A rush of bicycles brought the children back and then the youngest one came running down from the garage, she must come and look. Happy with the fee the afternoon's work would earn for her Mona joined them in the garden, at the compost heap, the neighbour of last night's fire. There, not exactly a rose in a dung-heap, but still so strange to see, was the frivolous tutu of a cyclamen, tiny, pink and pure. She explained to the waiting children about the forgotten corm, and the tolerant warmth of the compost, all weeds and scavengings, and even, perhaps, the catalyst of the bonfire. Science had the answers, they agreed, but her daughter thought there was more than this, the little plant had shown something else.

'Courage, perhaps?' Mona said it for her, calling it again a kind of lyrical determination. They looked together at the frail mesh of tissue, transparent now as the evening deepened, and Mona suddenly found the image in her mind – faith of our fathers, she thought: that was it – 'Faith of our fathers, Living still, In spite of dungeon, fire and sword.' Whatever about the sword, the poor little folded corm had found dungeon and fire in her back garden, but there it was, living still. Smiling together, they drifted back to chips for tea, and television, and preparations for another day.

From the Mainland

The voice that is thinking here is not a remembering voice; it is imagining. Imagining what is real, for memory surely feeds that part of the mind which sees, and turns what was into what might have been, what is into what may become.

First, then, there is the shock of reality on the hill above Westport. The white road, flanked by a white garage, a bungalow, tumbles from its course and crests the brow of the hill at a run. From there, taking time to slow down as the car skates into the drop, the visitor can see what has always been real to the eyes of the native. The massif of Clare Island rears from the sea, slate against pearl, a glittering silhouette, and illusion greater than its background, haloed by the sunfall on sea, the sea itself a limitless seam of silver silk stretching into coves, into inlets and sounds, with a rim of moving ice around the rocks which form its landward frame.

It is a picture viewed from a distance, viewed from the mainland. From that summit outside the town of Westport on the northern road it is possible also to see a fleck on the ridged screen of water: a moving freckle which transforms itself into a fishing smack, a Galway hooker with its sails folded or a boat made here on the island shores, trawling south towards Cleggan, fishing around Inishboffin and Clare. If its course is steady, wavering only as the watching eye blinks and waters in the glare, it may be the mailboat trudging its summer load to the beaches and monastic sites of the headlands which loom so black against the sun.

From the distance of this hill the rotund vessel becomes a caravel. From the mainland, the island peaks, their curved peninsulas mirrored again and again on the light that surrounds them, take on the mist of Hy Brasil. These are not waters for the white innocent sails of yachts. Even men who knew these creeks are buried in them, and the crafts of the sea have held the islanders together for centuries, accessible, but still remote. Remote enough, at least, to remain romantic, to appear mysterious. Clare itself presents a black monolithic face. It asserts itself as impassive, impenetrable, enigmatic. Alluring. The islands beyond it lie opaque with mystery; the ocean opens out beyond them too. Its transparencies offer islands again, like nebulae, shapes transient as cloud, actual as cloud, so that reality is obscured, and these light-ridden vaporous landfalls enter the imagination as seen, remembered. Real.

On a hill on one of the islands in this western archipelago a man blinked his eyelids against a tickle of winnowing hay and looked to the sea. He blinked again to identify the black craft surging towards the shore. Straightening his back by leaning against the braced pressure of his hand he looked down to the shingle and saw Paddy Con Pat and Neilie Manus pushing one of the currachs onto the tide, holding its lifting frame on the water until they saw the nearing boat come closer.

On the hill Eddie Mick Michael looked to the fields that lurched over the rocks below him. He saw the sharp glitter of scythes being laid down on the yellow grass, the men and children gathering in groups on the shores of the little patches of hay. If the women who worked there with them had stood up, they had bent again to their task, stooking and gleaning. The men began to move towards the path that ran down the mountain, the children going too, but the women stood and called the children back in quiet voices that were not disobeyed. A man turned quickly, as if angry, to a woman who stood near a gap in the wall of stones, but higher up on the hill their words could not be heard and the woman stooped again, silenced, while the man took a boy by the hand and walked quickly after his fellows, their dust blowing like smoke, a faded odourless incense, in their wake.

The boat was larger now, thrusting steadily into the bay, its movement discernible even from the height where Eddie Mick Michael was watching. He could see the ordinary event like a picture, like a painting. The curve of its frame leaned from the south, sloping from the shoulder of the Twelve Bens into the Sheefrey Mountains and then into the mass of Mweelrea itself above the white strands of Killadoon and Thallabawn. Through those ranges the hungry eye could pierce as far as the flower-studded turf of Rossadillisk; from there on the inland side the lustrous woods at Delphi yielded to the holy barren cone of Croagh Patrick, and Clew Bay spun round to the Partry Mountains until stopped in its wheel by cliffs at the edge of Achill.

From the mainland the sea lay like wine in this chalice of mountains. Born to it, knowing it, Eddie Mick Michael could gaze at it still, and his eyes drank before returning to the boat which had throbbed to a floating halt on the swell in the cove. There was a woman on deck. He saw the lash of fair hair. And a man in a suit, yellow hair again. No one else except Jimmy Con Pat at the wheel, and Miah O'Malley as his mate. It was the ferry, out of its time. He saw the men from the hill fields meet the husband of the postmistress on the street, the nurse's husband, the teacher from the boys' school – the new school the island had never expected to need. The men had gathered, and the children, and at last Eddie Mick Michael threw down his scythe, not caring where the honed blade fell. He began to run, busy as he went, rolling down the sleeves of his shirt, buttoning the sweat-rimmed collar, plunging his arms into the thick sleeves of the jacket he had picked off its perch on the ditch. He ran noticing the vigour in his gait, the ease of his leaping feet as he cut across the turf-tightened boulders of the slope and jumped the two walls that held in the potato ridges drilled by Neilie Manus.

The tide was low. The men had sent out two currachs to the boat, and these nestled against its dirty side while the woman with her hair streaked silver and gold and the man in the black suit got into one of them, uneasily. The oarsmen pushed with their hands against the boat to get away before settling to the smooth rhythm of their rowing, hand lifting oar over hand, the craft riding the delicate waves until it was beached by the waves themselves, dry on the high edge of the shore.

The black dome of the priest's car stopped at the sea-wall, and hot in his black uniform Fr McGuinness stumbled across the stones to the visitors, his hand out to welcome, to console. Standing and sweating at the back of the waiting group of men Eddie saw the woman shake her yellow head and look down at the hard pebbles of the strand. But the man grasped the priest's hand, and held it, although Eddie could not see that they said anything to each other.

Two men from the crowd joined the rowers of the currach which was about to set back to the ferry, and when they reached it they climbed the rope ladder and disappeared. Eddie watched, aware that his heart was limping. Ropes dangling over the hold on the boat could be seen to tighten, to twist. The rowers waited on the waves, and Jimmy Con Pat and Miah O'Malley came up on deck and went to haul on the lines, and the men who had also gone below came up slowly, their backs to the boards, pushing with their hands the long weight which gleamed smooth and brandy-brown in the suddenly too-bright sun. The load swung free of their ballast and lifted, and the men on the deck shouted to the men alongside and caught at the ropes again and steadied and turned the burden to the side. It lurched and seemed about to slide; the men shouted in desperation and warning and spread the ropes and braced themselves, legs against timbers, for the slow careful drop into the currach beneath, where the oarsmen stood calmly on the lathes, riding the water, waiting to lengthen the lines and winch the coffin into the narrow basket of their boat.

Eddie was praying: *take care. Take care of her. She feared the sea so much – take care.* He knew, as all the watchers knew, that the men on the sea were not omnipotent. They had learned boats and the sea with the first breath they drew, but were not accustomed to such cargoes as this. Only people who died on the island were buried on the island, and the islanders died at home, or in America. Paddy Con Pat could have put out a brighter boat, a painted, engined, sea-faring vessel, but for this cargo they had left the new launches at their moorings and used what their fathers would have used – what they would have used, before the time that had come to be known as Mrs Dauntry's time.

It was not for her fear of the sea that the new boats had been brought in to the island: they had come with the drying plant, with the wool-house, with the marine biology centre. The pretty boats were there to take tourists on cautious fair-weather visits to the western shingles, and the seal-rocks, and Mrs Dauntry had never gone in them, doubting the littleness of skill they encouraged, the confidence they allowed. So on this day the narrow black boats had gone out for her, as on the day she first came to the island, as on the day she came back to make it her home.

There was a murmur on the beach as if all their watching prayers had been let slip in thankfulness when the coffin settled into the currach. The boat began to move slowly, heavily to the land, shepherded by the men in the second currach, matching its pace to keep it company. At the shore the loaded boat could not mount the shingle, and men rushed to pull it from the shallows and it shuddered across the slick weed and greasy pebbles at the edge of the tide.

'Go easy! She'll rip!' Paddy Con Pat shouted, and the

179

men flexed themselves and shouldered the currach and coffin together. They stumbled to that point on the beach where the priest stood, and many hands fumbled for a hold on the ropes, lifting the coffin from the boat and laying it smoothly on the strand. The nurse came out of the white-painted dispensary and rushed across the road to the beach, a bunch of flowers in her big hand. She was the only woman there except for that girl who stood apart from them all, even from the young man who was her brother, now that Eddie recognized them both. They were not strangers to the island, for all their strangeness now. Their strangeness was the oddity felt by everyone on the beach. They were all foundered, not even Fr McGuinness knew what to do next.

Nurse Brown broke from the ruck of people and put her flowers on the centre of the coffin, exactly where the crucifix should have been, and turned to the priest.

'All the same, Father Mac, I think we should have a prayer.'

Behind her the silent group stirred, and hands searched Rosary Beads from pockets. The children crossed themselves while the priest took his purple stole from his jacket and kissed it. After a hesitant glance at Nurse Brown, a sideways look at the bent head of the girl at the edge of the crowd, he began the Lord's Prayer.

There was tact in that, Eddie Mick Michael knew, but he did not join in the voices. He wondered if the priest had meant to slow and lengthen the words about forgiveness and trespasses, and he saw how the girl lifted her blonde head at that moment, alert for meanings, before the phrases took back their rhythms.

Not looking at her he remembered how she had come down the steps between the fuchsia bushes, much younger then, of course, and lovely, the swathe of glossy hair as bright as July meadow-grass. They had met where only one could pass on the slabs, she going down from the house, he going up, his fingers spiked with mackerel. She had looked at him. He saw in her bright defiant eyes the anger of suspicion, of reckless dislike. He stood away from her to let her get beyond him, but as her body brushed against his she had turned briefly back, and narrowed her eyes and tightened her mouth. She hissed the words at him –

'You don't think you're the only one, do you? There's never only one – not even here!'

Before he could catch the words securely she had jumped over the next step downwards and was running across the little bawn below the house until hidden by rock. Where had she gone to, to hide, he wondered now, when it was too late to help her find a holt, and she stood exposed on the beach, grieving, but ashamed.

'She'll always be ashamed of me,' Mrs Dauntry had explained her daughter when Eddie told her about the meeting on the steps, the spurted words.

'She can't help it, she's young, and her father was ashamed of me too, so I suppose she thinks she's doing the right thing.'

Her tone was easy, unaddressed. He had imagined she would understand the accusation the girl had made. It had taken him minutes to understand – not the only one, never the only one—

'Am I the only one?' He asked it straight away when he came in the door, and she had understood.

'Yes.' She had answered without hesitation, giving him the word he wanted. Then she had smiled, and it was the smile that he had carried with him from that question and that answer too, and quelled the first rising of the feeling that should have come later, the feeling that young girl knew about, knew how to provoke.

Why had he not been jealous? Why had there been no sense of humiliation, not even under the lash of the girl's taunt? Because he must have known. He had smelt tobacco smoke there in her kitchen where he had no pipe, nor she cigarettes. It was not the voluptuous odour of cigars left by some of her friends from the mainland, but the reek of familiar men, men he knew.

'Billy Burke is making very free with that Mrs

181

Dauntry,' his mother said crisply one day, watching the tall young fisherman carrying lobsters in a creel up the hill to the house Mrs Dauntry had taken, its back to the village. It was not long after that, when Eddie thought about it, that Billy Burke had bought the engine for his boat, and not long after that either that the summer priest had married him to a girl who came into the island from Murrisk, where she had been working in a guest-house.

'Are you making free with me?' Mrs Dauntry had asked him in bed, in her bed curved like a ship, the laugh in her voice licensing him to say that he would want to be making free with her again, and again, and again, his voice muffled in her hair.

'What would your mother say?' She was teasing him, but he knew it was something to be thought about. He knew that he carried home with him the evidence of her house, of the strong twisting smell of turpentine and the languorous coil of pigmented oils. No one could see the names in his brain but he uttered them to himself, perhaps aloud: yellow ochre, burnt umber, vermilion, crimson lake. He knew then that there were inks that were not for writing, he saw brushes fine as an eyelash, he held pastel colour in a chalk in his hand and saw it crumble with casual pressure, leaving a pale dust, downy as a moth.

It was not that he was learning anything that could be put to use for himself. She was not educating him, there was no conscious process of exchange in their relationship. He saw one night that the book she had put down when he came in was called *Ring of Bright Water*. When, attracted by the title, he asked her what it was about, she said it was a story of a man and an otter and the sea, but she did not offer it to him to read for himself and so he never did. Yet he carried the title home with him like a vision. If she gave him anything, perhaps that was it, a way of seeing things, even the familiar could become strangely beautiful if looked at through her lenses.

He was stirred by her certainties. He had realized with a pleasure that had an ache to it that he had come to see what she could show, that he could look at the cropped colours of the pasture and put a shape around them. On the driftwood mantel above her fireplace a friend who called himself a stone-cutter had put a curve of grey stone. When Eddie lifted it his palm felt it sleek as a salmon and his skin dampened with recognition; this was not a new satisfaction. His flesh became alert to significance he could not understand, he was content not to understand. Instead he made a picture in his soul of what there was to see, even when he watched her almost absently, seeing her pull gently, dreamily at the ears of a donkey she had called to the ditch. He heard and remembered how her voice caressed the beast, he saw forever how the animal lowered its head and accepted her consoling hand against the greasy hair of its neck. And the picture could stretch to show the squat brown dog she called Toby whining in frantic jealousy yet ready, the minute she walked on, to forgive her all her adulteries.

'You have given me something,' he told her once, answering the question he was not to ask for many years. That answer had come at a time when their special friendliness was drawing to an easy close, and he was recognizing the possibilities of his own life.

'You have given me something of yourself, a thing I can't put a name to. Maybe you have only made me want things, or want to be able to have what I want, just as you have what you want.'

He had wanted to say to her, he had begun to try to say, that she had given him pleasure. That was the simple thing. But she had also given him the knowledge that he pleased her – that was new. When he first saw her naked he told her, when he could speak, that she looked like a photograph of a statue he had seen once in the Doctor's house in Clifden, when he had brought his mother out there for that trouble with her eyes. It was not until he saw the other pictures, the pictures that she painted, that he understood what he looked like, the white block of his body emerging from flowered shadow, the softly mottled globes of his sex lying like strawberries on the stubble of his hair. So there was that much more to it – not only the sense of wanting, but of being. He could not explain this to her, he had no words for it, then.

As he saw her now Eddie thought that Mrs Dauntry's daughter might be absolved of her desire to harm. If she could not meet the eyes of the people assembled here, people who looked at her with kindness and pity, was it perhaps because she was ashamed, not of her mother, but of herself? Perhaps she remembered how the peace of those days of her mother's life on the island had been offered to her, as to her brother. The boy had accepted and outgrown it and stood here now acknowledging the comfort that was being offered, knowing the truth of what was not being said. It was memory which was working in her, not her imagination. In youth it is imagination, the temptation to think the worst, or the best, which makes life unbearable; later it is the memory of what really happened which sears at each recall, and for this girl there had been no one yet to help her graft another skin over the scar. No one except her mother, who had not tried to heal, although she had witnessed the wounding.

As the prayer ended the group broke up again, separate as stones, and without much confusion drew Mrs Dauntry's son into their pattern as the men lifted the coffin to their shoulders. As a man among these men he walked as steadily as they did beneath the burden, up onto the road, making for the back of the hill and the only north-facing cottage on the island, its slated roof broken by two skylights which the people had said would let the weather into the loft, but that hadn't happened, the work was well done, the men had skills they had had no use for until those windows were required.

Eddie Mick Michael saw how one of the bearers put

up a quick hand to settle the flowers on the coffin, but they slid and fell to the ground as the steps were gained and the red and purple petals of the fuchsia brushed like flowered rain on the casket. He caught the bundle before the followers could tread on the distillation of its colours, and saw the care with which stout Nurse Brown had composed it. The bold bright dog-daisies supported the blue essence of harebells, stalks of sea-lavender were almost hidden by the tender hairy scabious and campion, by the long bearded grasses gathered from the heavy edges of the island's fields.

He knew the names now – but then he had always known them, discovering that truth to his own surprise when she had asked him about the weeds, the spurge and trefoil, the slanlús. When he brought her to where they were growing, or when she found them, as one day she found a great cliff-top fringe of sea-thrift bursting like pink spray against the sky, then she would sit on the turf among the rabbit-holes and look, and look, as if she could breathe their very being into her blood-stream. As the flowers wilted beneath his hand he saw the translucent arc of her fingernail numbering the ambrosial petals of the wild woodbine, and felt as he had felt once in the walled shelter of her garden her clutch on his sleeve, silencing him to watch a bee stirring the filaments of a panniered poppy by the very susurration of its wings.

It had mystified him that she could perceive all these simple things and in that perception give them importance. And the people who came to visit her, walking on the grassy shingles of the beaches to see the tern, striding the cliffs to watch the fulmar, or at other seasons rowing to Inishturc to count migrating geese, spending weeks there, or camping with cameras and notebooks and bits of machinery above the rocks so big and so far off the shore to be almost islands themselves, where the seals fought and mated and gave birth; these people too were a wonder to the islanders.

Yet, like Mrs Dauntry, they had recognized things on

185

the island which had always been there. The few remaining fishermen of those first days of her living there had spoken of the seals with scorn, for in damaging the fishing they were a source of poverty while somehow retaining an uncomfortable flavour of superstition. And geese were the only visitors on Inishturc now that the prople had left it – as indeed, the men said and the women praised them for saying it, the people would leave this island too, soon.

Eddie Mick Michael would have said the same. With two brothers in Chicago urging him to emigrate, with nothing to live on but his boat and a few fields and the government's dole, without a woman of his own as most of the young men left on the island were without a woman, perhaps he had already stayed too long. It had been three years since there had been a christening on the island, and that child's mother was dead within six months of its birth. There would be no priest soon, the plan was to keep a curate there from late spring to early autumn. The girls went off young to schools in Galway or Clifden or Westport and grew up at a distance from their homes, and the boys too went away and learned skills and trades and went on to Dublin or Manchester or Massachusetts. They did not come back to the island, before Mrs Dauntry's time.

There was not much left to island life when Mrs Dauntry came. Eddie Mick Michael had not been there to see that arrival, nor had he seen her on her earlier visit although he had heard talk of her in the post office, and heard that she had been invited to an American wake for the two Joyce brothers. He had gone to the Joyce house on that evening but had not seen her. The farewells weighted his consciousness. He did not like the way the old people – for he had been a young man then – looked at him and said they supposed it wouldn't be long before he'd be on the same road himself. They sucked their pipes and reminded one another that there wasn't a woman under thirty nearer than Louisburgh and that there was only one unmarried

186

woman between thirty and forty and she was half mad already. When he had shaken Peter Joyce's hand and thrown his arm without words around Danny Joyce's shoulder, he had gone back the road to the village and spent the rest of the night in the public house.

He was not a drinker, but he got drunk that night, and stayed drunk for most of the following winter, sober only for those times in the days when he had to feed his few lean black cattle and not always then. His mother tried to scold him but she was afraid, knowing that a reckoning was being made, and she kept to her hens and her knitting until she heard that there was work for sale at the house on the hill, the house taken by that Mrs Dauntry who would be coming back to the island in the spring.

There was money being spent there, and no mistake! The big room that was the kitchen in every cottage on the island was getting a new floor and polished timbers were to be laid on this; timber panelling was to be put against all the walls of the room beyond that and another wooden floor laid down. There was to be a windowed porch sheltering the front door, and the rocky path outside it was to be hewn into steps, evenly placed and banked to take the harm out of the steep slope.

There was building going on at the back, where there was to be a bathroom, and a plumber was bringing some men over from Cleggan for the digging and lining and fitting of a septic tank – a 'cess-pit', Eddie's mother had said when the women talked about it among themselves – and the installation of a pump for water. The derelict sheds outside were to be roofed and cleaned and a bit of the bog leased to supply turf. No instructions had been given about the big black range built into the kitchen wall next to the wide fireplace, but Eddie's mother said she had a feeling it would be wanted and to leave it alone until Mrs Dauntry saw it again. In the meantime she polished it to shining self-justification and saw that it was in working order. Great round canisters of gas were being brought over

187

on the boat whose cargoes were unloaded before a growing audience – it was winter, there was not much else to watch. Eddie talked with the carpenter who came down from Dublin in the first mild days of spring to put in shelves for what he said would be a world of books and, to the wonder of all that saw the finished article, to build a bed under the window in the new-panelled back room. It was more like a boat than a bed, the men told themselves, with the curved headboard like a scroll turning away from where the bolster would be and the foot folding over in a wheel of wood which fitted into a projection of the panelling.

It was all great for talk, and speculation – 'that's a big bed for one woman!' they said, accepting the suggestion of Mrs Dauntry's widowhood. For Eddie, the wonder of it all was in the loft, where the new floor-boards had a kind of golden gloss, matching the timber lining of the walls and catching all the clean white light that poured in through the two windows in the roof, set with slanting glass brought over from Westport. The Dublin carpenter said that the light was important for painting and seeing Eddie's incomprehension added that Mrs Dauntry was a painter of pictures. But what was there to paint on the island, Eddie wondered, and the carpenter said he didn't know, but perhaps she carried the pictures around in her head, wherever she was.

'I don't know, really,' she had said, some doubt in her answer when he put the question to her.

'No – I *do* know. It's just that I can't explain it.'

Because he sat silent, waiting, she added quickly to help him:

'It's not like that for everyone. It's not that there's any secret world that anyone is shut out of. I mean it's like your eye. Your eye either focuses in, sees something very sharply, recognizes it, and can reproduce it, exactly, although still only in your mind; or your eye diffuses the object, you see something with all your eyes, all the fuzzy bits, the things that hint at a smell, or a feel, and you can paint that, too, or instead.'

She said: 'So maybe it is like a secret after all. It's a way of seeing, and when you paint, and people understand what you saw, it's as though they share the secret with you.'

So that was the secret of his body – except that it was not a secret. It was not even his body that he saw ribbed by her pencil – perhaps it was Billy Burke or Tom Joe Bracken who had sat with her quietly down in the pub those few nights before going away to England. If they saw the pictures did they see themselves – or him? Or in the flowers which flowed like coloured water on the thick, dimpled paper; did these glistening paintings, limpid with the tints of thrift and scabious and dense purple heather – did they yield up their secrets to the widened, remembering eye? And why was there no jealousy in this?

It was *Because*. Because when he looked at the shape of an etched, pinioned leaf transformed on her canvas to something more than photo synthesis, the picture had a thick, sudden smell to it, and the light boring through the roof of the loft was hot and eager and crushed the essence of wild thyme and clover under his back as they rested together that day at Rossadillisk and he felt as if the heat of their love-making had soaked damply into the welcoming turf. That was the leaf's message to him, a green energy fused into his soul through his mind's eye. That was his, that leaf, vibrant on the easel's plank. What others saw was theirs, their secret, their own escape into the painting's mystery.

That explained, too, why people would pay such big money for Mrs Dauntry's work, she called it work, and all the people of the island who knew her began to do so. What else was there to call something that took her out in the fields at night, or to the North Cliffs in a morning mist so thick that the sheep did not see her and were not afraid? Because she did those things, lost in them and still somehow responsive to the greetings of anyone who met her, and because she was paid for what she

189

produced as a result, it was known to be work like work on the land. Eddie had seen the prices paid in a catalogue he found in her studio after her return from a trip to Dublin. Bringing it home to show his mother, he earned at last her respect for Mrs Dauntry, and he knew that the nice big numbers of pounds would be repeated among the island women until they lost their suspicion of her ways.

'Wouldn't you think, now,' his mother wondered, 'that she'd live somewhere else, where there'd be lots of things for her to make pictures of?'

There was no point, he knew, in talking to her about secrets, or about the ways of seeing. But his mother had liked the smooth photographs in the catalogue and praised their shine, and had no further curiosity.

He had said to Mrs Dauntry –

'Herself won't come over to the house with me to see some of your pictures. But she likes the photographs I showed her. She thinks you must be very able.'

Mrs Dauntry hadn't laughed. They were sitting at the length of the white deal table in the kitchen, where the light fell sharp and cold, his hand splayed out limp on a clean cloth while she tried to extract a splinter of broken timber from underneath the flesh of his palm. It had taken days for the seal of skin to redden over the thin, purple wound; he had ignored it until he winced in her hearing when he had taken up the axe to chop blocks for her fire.

It was the kind of hurt he was used to in a life of stings and grazes and cuts, the casual injuries of farming. The little black stick would have worked its way through his skin, he had seen it happen before, it would break through its cushion of hot, hardened blood like a hair, and he would work it out with his finger and rinse off the yellowish fluid which followed it in sea-water. But he liked her ways with him. He liked the light hold of her hand on his, and the bright striped towel under his knuckles, and the heat of her poultice on his straining skin.

190

She was frowning when he told her about his mother, frowning in case she might hurt him while she pressed against the reluctant sliver. It was hurting him in fact a lot more than it would if left alone for another few days when, he knew without fear of the poison she spoke of, it would emerge in its own time. But he did not tell her this.

'My mother thinks you must be very able,' he said again to tease her.

'So I am able.'

She spoke without lifting her head. Her hair was dark brown with grey growing through it. He had never asked her how old she was, but she was older than him by about fifteen years; he knew that from her daughter who was in her early teens when Mrs Dauntry first came to the island. Her son had been away at the college then, living in Dublin, where the daughter went to school. Mrs Dauntry lived in the house by herself, and even when the boy and girl came there on holidays, they seemed to Eddie to be different from her other guests only in that they stayed with her for a longer time.

'So. I. Am. Able!' With each punctuated word she drew further on to his palm the wicked little spike. Triumphant, she swabbed and dried the wound and pressed the sticking-plaster across it. One hand still lying on his outstretched fingers, she held the tweezers up to the light, considering the tiny spear they held.

'They're the only things I miss,' her eyes creased against the shine.

'Trees. I miss them. Not just the look of them, not just the feel of the bark, like a crust, or the cycle of leaves. But the sound of them. Here, sometimes, I have imagined them. The rain on the bushes. And the wind. I was so used to trees. It was like being able to tell the time by them – the times of your life.'

'You could go back down to Delphi for a little while,' he said, anxious for her desire.

'The woods there are grand. Wouldn't they suit you? Or you could go over to Westport. Or beyond Cleggan,

191

near Clifden, there's a Planter's house. It's a ruin now, but the woods are all around it still. And no one goes there. You could be alone.'

He heard his voice going on, offering, propitiating. He wanted to keep talking, for she had begun to move her hand slowly on his without looking at what she was doing. He could feel that her mind had gone away from what they were saying, gone into that question they had all asked, every one of them on the island had asked, what was she doing here. They had never asked *her*, but he had seen how when the talk in the pub was about places elsewhere there would be a different shade in her silence. He knew, she had told him herself, that she had no hunger for Dublin or London or even the cities of Europe or America. She had been there, lived in them, some of them were still the commonplaces of her working life, demanding brief journeys, yielding money and letters and in summer so many visitors that two island housewives had had to help accommodate them and as a result had begun a little bed and breakfast business of their own.

It was not the tourists that made her think of somewhere away from the island, nor the guests who all accepted now that the island was her home. She had that power, Eddie realized long ago; when a thing became absolute for her, as it did with her work, as it did with her life on the island, it became absolute too for those who had to deal with her. It was a power of silent assertion. Thus the island was her home, the only possible challenge would have had to be from the islanders themselves, and they had not challenged her.

That might have been a queer thing, if there had been any talk. They would have wondered why it was they did not dismiss her as other migrants had been ignored or tolerated, remembered only as part of a joke against the people of the mainland cities. It might be that Mrs Dauntry was a wonder in herself, offering no explanations, making no demands, promising nothing, extracting nothing, questioning nothing. Questioning nothing

192

except how to get her turf dry enough for the range, touching their experience only where it was of value to her. They were not eccentrics, not curiosities to her, and her coming had displaced nobody.

Eddie had heard her daughter scoff:

'Your own generator! Why are you here, so – you're not trying to live like the people here! You're importing your own style of life, and changing nothing for other people – you could be doing that anywhere!'

Mrs Dauntry did not defend herself. She seemed to love this girl who scorned her, and was not angry.

'Yes,' she agreed, in the calm voice she always used for her daughter.

'I *am* importing what I want. Some of the things I want from my life are here already, I bring in what I want of what's missing. I think that's fair enough.'

'But you benefit only yourself! You're taking the atmosphere of this place, you're using it for your work – but what are you giving back? What are you doing for anyone here?'

Mrs Dauntry took her hands from the dough she was kneading and looked at her daughter as if she were something she was going to paint. She had never done that, with either of her children; she had no portraits of them. She herself had created some of the secrets of their lives, and would not expose them.

'You're so full of energy, Ruth. It's not always a matter of doing things, of being active and harried and demanding. Sometimes you can just let things be. I don't want to change anything here. Perhaps things should be changed, but not by me. The island is itself, the people are themselves. They don't want me to give them anything. Whatever happens here will happen out of some kind of fusion of all of us. And we must wait for it to happen, whether for good or for bad.'

The girl looked across at Eddie who stood by the sink, his knife slitting the glittering fish that heaped on the drainer.

'How can they be content to wait?' She was not

193

asking him. 'What kind of people are they, not to try and get the things they need to keep on living here?'

The scorn in her voice was for him too.

'Well, people don't always know what it is they want. Until they see it, perhaps used by someone elsewhere. And people don't always know what they see, either. Sometimes you have to learn how to see.'

Mrs Dauntry too looked at Eddie, with a smile in her eyes which was not there when she looked at her daughter.

'But Ruth,' she added then, 'you know that I have come here only for myself. You must not keep coming over if it upsets you so much. You must not come if it only makes you angry, and impatient. That anger might be more useful somewhere other than here. It's good anger, good energy – it should be put to good use.'

'Dermot comes,' Ruth answered. Her brother's casual, accepting visits to the island always irked her. He was her friend but could not share her grievance.

Mrs Dauntry seemed to sigh, but made no sound with it.

'Dermot takes what suits him from life. He comes to the island when he needs it, perhaps when he needs me, I don't know. He likes what he finds here, he puts no effort into it, makes no demands. What isn't here, what he needs, he brings with him.'

'Like his girl-friends,' Ruth said, suddenly, sharply, and then laughed, and they all laughed, remembering Dermot's girl-friends and their high-heeled sandals and their swimsuits and their incapability which endeared them briefly to the people of the island.

Eddie liked Dermot. He liked him because there was something both casual and manly in his affection for Mrs Dauntry, and because he made her laugh, even when she talked to him about her will, and the house in Dublin he shared with Ruth. And there was never anything in Dermot's behaviour to make Eddie think the young man knew about Mrs Dauntry's ways with men.

194

Even with Dermot himself she could be sexual. There was some ingredient in her motherhood of a male which stirred her sexuality. Eddie saw it in the languorous hand with which she stroked her son's hair, and in Dermot's accommodating response, as if her caresses had followed him into manhood, changing their tender emphasis as his masculinity strengthened.

With her daughter too Mrs Dauntry had this physical attentiveness. If they stood or sat closely together, even in public, she would make as if to catch the girl's hand, and once he had seen them both on the strand, fingers reaching fingers from each outstretched arm as they poised like balances for one another on the slithering rocks. And there was a photograph on the bedroom wall in the house – he could never let on to Ruth that he had seen it – in which Mrs Dauntry swung between the shoulders of her two tall children, an arm on each of them, all three of them glinting with unshadowed laughter and the sun making haloes of their hair.

The light from the quartered window was dimming now, but Mrs Dauntry's palm rested on Eddie's upturned fingers, his palm under hers. He felt her skin tremble. It was not soft or smooth, the skin of her hand, not like the white hands of the women in stories. The summer brown had paled from it now, it had a weathered look, not rough like his own but with a smoother hardness, although her palm felt rounded and full against his fingers, and her skin flickered where it touched him.

As though it were a pulse which brought her back to life she moved, but did not move away.

'No, I won't go down to Delphi. Not just yet. Later, in the winter when the trees are bare. I'd like to admire them then, to share their cold.'

But the seas would be rough in winter, and even in calm weather she did not like the crossing to the mainland. Eddie wondered at her.

'And I won't go to the Planter's house. I hate that

word – *Planter*. The Plantations were so long ago. They were in the time of Elizabeth the First, they did no harm to us. And surely the woods are innocent – why do the people of Clifden still hate that house?'

Eddie did not know. A child of his generation, he had never doubted that it was right for the Planter's house to be in ruins, unsellable. Yes, it was an old hurt, and he looked down at the new blemish on his skin. He made a quick cage of his two hands, trapping hers.

'I'm thankful to you, Madam.' He used the whole word. He had heard a man from France say it to her once, *Ma Dame*, and had watched her blush with pleasure. Her eyes gleamed with surprise as he held her there at the table, as he shortened the word without awkwardness.

'I'm grateful to you for removing that little sleá for me. The little splinter. You like to take splinters out of people's lives for them, don't you?'

'Do I, Eddie?' She slid her hand gently out of his.

'Maybe that's what it looks like.' But he had surprised her and he knew it, and even as she began to put away the bowl of cooling water and the towel and tweezers, he saw there was a sudden awkwardness in her speech with him, that he had touched something almost unseen, and unsettled her, and he felt a new awareness of himself.

He had been there that day to chop her bits of wood. He did jobs like that for her. All the men did. She had employed one of them to build a garden for her, once. The Garden, it had become. The bawn on the southern slope of her two acres had been cut to the clay and the slide down had been held by terraces. Where the ground was exposed to the wind a wall had been made from two thicknesses of stones brought up by anyone who happened to be passing – mostly by the few children left on the island. Then the wall had been bridled itself, and shrubs saddled it, and fruit bushes flourished on the manure of the black cows. The men helped her dig it and saw how young vegetables grew for her under

196

hoops of transparent plastic. Some of the women came up to see The Garden as it grew and though they walked all round it with Mrs Dauntry it was among themselves they talked.

Eddie Mick Michael had wondered what the Madam would do with the rest of the bawn. She talked one night in the public house about the growing awareness of the value of goat's milk but it was Neilie Manus who brought over the pair of goats to graze on his own patches of rocky bog. And another time when she asked in the post office if anyone on the island did much in the way of knitting it wasn't for herself she wanted the ganseys but for a woman with a different kind of shop in Dublin. It turned out that the woman herself came to the island with a man who looked at some of the sheep and spoke to some of the older women.

So when there began to be odd bits of talk, and more sheep were brought to the island, and some of the older women took up their almost forgotten task of carding, and gradually the island began to sell something it had produced itself, none of it had anything to do with Mrs Dauntry. She instructed no one except about what she wanted for herself.

'That's what I want in a garden,' she told Eddie one evening – 'blackcurrant bushes, and hens! That's what my grandmother had in her garden, once.'

There was more than that, over the years. Tentative roses held to the white walls, and hollyhocks frilled in the corners. When she got her generator and put in a freezer, she grew more vegetables, more luscious fruit. She made jam, her early mornings in summer spent picking what could be preserved, her evenings boiling and bottling, or mixing the fruit with cheese made from the goats' milk. Some of the older men had sons who came in from Galway and Mayo and brought their young wives with them to work on the island. Their industry was not casual; it began to happen that they considered other ways, other possibilities. The men and women who came to visit Mrs Dauntry met the islanders in the pub, or on the beaches among the boats. They talked of fishing, boat-building, and of special catches, unique skills.

A fat man who explained that he was a Professor of Botany at a University in England went walking with Eddie Mick Michael one morning, one summer, to the high fields. The cut grass left lying in the stubble to dry glistened like green polish, and the basking crows held their wings out from their sides, as if trying to sit in their own shade. They were not what the Professor wanted to see, but the dim flowers which bloomed at the fields' edges, which he had seen blooming on canvas and paper in Mrs Dauntry's house.

Even the common flowers were of interest to this Professor. He was not the island's first academic, even before Mrs Dauntry learned men had come there, to scan the birds, to break rocks into shards, to name and measure the tumbled ruin of the little monastic church. With Eddie as his company and guide this Professor panted as he wrote the Latin names into a small black book; the hill on this warmer southern side was steep, but the walk along the highest bogs brought them gradually down again, stopping to look, stopping to write, and Eddie wondered why she had not come with them, knowing how much she cared for this little man, how ardent she was for the shy flowers he sought. They came to a halt together, their booted feet hidden by heather.

'Been bad, these last few weeks, has she?'

The Professor's question had startled Eddie, he had no answer. He had noticed her shelling pills like peas from a bottle, and one night not long since there had been a violent violet edge to her mouth. He could not give this evidence aloud.

'Only to be expected. Another operation, I'd say. Told her she should go to London. Only place. Know a man in Guys, the best. Tell her I said so, sometime, will you? Only not too long, don't wait too long.'

Eddie knew he could not tell Mrs Dauntry anything

198

about herself, what she should do. This man's shy, breathless injunction made only a little sense, for yes, she had been bad, they had all known she was not herself, everyone on the island knew because she had asked Billy Burke's two sons to help her in the garden, and his wife had taken the gooseberries and black-currants down to her house to make Mrs Dauntry's jam.

The priest who now lived all year long on the island was an elderly man, and mild. Although Mrs Dauntry would never go to Mass or attend the Sacraments, his car could be seen by her house sometimes, and it had been noticed lately that his visits were more frequent. The women, those who in earlier days had caught Mrs Dauntry's smell from their men, or who had perhaps been told by a husband what it was that turned his mind to marrying, those women had said then that Mrs Dauntry was going to turn, that Fr McGuinness was bringing her back to the church at last, and only just in time.

It was not that the women disliked her. Perhaps they feared her. When the island had had a summer priest only it was known that a woman had gone to him and told him things about Mrs Dauntry. The island had agreed that the woman had been simple, astray after the misery of a miscarriage, afraid that her husband would leave her if she was barren, although such a thing had never been known to happen on the island. She was not an island woman, and could be forgiven for trying to bring Mrs Dauntry's name down. And all the island knew what Fr McGuinness had said once to a fearful young wife who had been told by another woman about Mrs Dauntry and the men:

'I don't mind where he gets his appetite,' the priest told her kindly, 'so long as he eats at home.'

It was true, for the last few years of her life on the island, that Mrs Dauntry had no lovers among the local men. They knew her and they respected her, and if they recognized that they had shared her among themselves, and with men who came from the mainland, they did not go to the priest about it, for what would they be confessing but only someone else's sins? And what need was there anyway to worry about what was past and gone? Weren't there women enough on the island now? And children?

It was the very same Professor that got an order from England for Mrs Dauntry to draw and colour the pictures for a seed catalogue. Some time after that another man came and there was talk of harvesting the wild flowers, and that was the beginning of the drying shed for seeds, and students from the University in Galway came to the island for part of their studies. The people of the island were not people to look too far ahead, but it had been said quietly among them that it would not be long before some of their own children were among the students from the University, especially now that the new school was to be built.

Ruth had been at University, Eddie knew. She had left her studies only weeks before sitting for an important examination. She had not told Mrs Dauntry then. It was Dermot who had brought the news, incidental to his own purpose on a holiday visit. Eddie met Mrs Dauntry and her son at the party held to celebrate the return to the island of the Joyce brothers. When she wanted to leave before Dermot was inclined to go, Eddie offered to walk to the house with her, and she took his arm as they went out together.

'It's a good night for the Joyces.' Eddie knew something was wrong, he wanted to break her silence. It was spring and the night was dusky, the air still sharp but smelling of promise.

They stopped where the road came out on the cliff and looked at the darkness of the sea, still brighter than the darkness of the land. Over Westport clouds burned like raw sienna and Eddie felt the lights of the town were growing dimmer, less inescapable.

'It's good to see the men coming back to the island. The life coming back to it. Dan Joyce, he's a proud and happy man tonight to be the father of those two men. And his wife, to be their mother.'

'They may go away again.' Mrs Dauntry's voice was light.

'Not everyone can stick with what they think they want to do. Things may go wrong here. What if they can't find a woman to marry, or the land goes against them? Will their mother still be proud, will she be happy then?'

He was not used to hearing her speak with the anxious sadness he heard now.

'What mother wouldn't be proud to have reared a pair of men like them? And part of the pride would be in letting them go, letting them do what they thought best for themselves, I mean – that's what you raise them for, isn't it? To look after themselves?'

He put an arm around her shoulders, comforting her with shelter. She leaned her head backwards against his body; in the blue haze of starlight he could see where her hair shone silver.

'Ruth says she won't finish her degree. She won't graduate, she won't sit her exams. She has gone to France, I don't know where.'

'But she's not a child. Even at the University she was a mature student, wasn't she? I mean she's an adult, she must be allowed to run her own life.'

'Yes. If I could feel that's what she's doing, instead of drifting. She's just drifting. It's such a waste of all that she is, what she could be. Such a failure.'

When he did not respond she answered her own question.

'My failure, I think. I should have married her father. I did want her, and I didn't want him, then. I never thought that she would want him. That was the thing I couldn't give her, and nothing else would do.'

Eddie could accept all this, but he had not wanted to hear it. He slackened the hold of his arm, and she laughed sharply.

'You're not shocked, are you? I never made any

secret of the way I lived. Certainly nobody here objected too loudly!'

There was a tension in his silence, and she repented.

'I'm sorry, Eddie. The truth is that this is the only place where there was no objection. It's why I stayed, the acceptance, and the kindness of the love I was given here. There was no insistence that I must change, or I must marry, or just be for one man alone. None of that. No demands for what I couldn't be, or give. It was as if I'd been given some special kind of licence, permitting me to be only what I am.'

Aching to hear her talk of him, Eddie said only –

'Perhaps that's what Ruth wants, too.'

He felt her shake her head.

'No. She has that. Dermot has that. I've said to myself, perhaps it's that she doesn't know who she is, and has not yet got the courage to find out. She doesn't see that life can be an adventure, and yet she lives very dangerously. There's something else. I think she wants to have had a different kind of past. There is nothing, *nothing*, I can do about it.'

She was letting the sadness go. She straightened from his arm and turned into him. He could see how her eyes gleamed as she looked up at him.

'And you, Eddie? What about you? Do you want to have had a different past?'

There was something a little more than teasing in the way she said the words. She had put both her hands under his jacket, she was drawing herself closer to him. He could feel her elbows through the soft dim wool she wore, and his body lurched with expectation as he thought of his answer.

'Not any more,' he said. It was enough.

It was Dermot who came to take Mrs Dauntry to the hospital in Dublin. When word got around the island there had been some plan for a leave-taking, a gathering of those who could now call themselves her old friends, although some of them had only come to live on the island in the last five years or so. She heard of it,

202

and wouldn't let it happen. Apart from Mrs O'Malley at the post office and Nurse Brown in the dispensary there wouldn't be another woman willing to enter her house, and the news that their husbands would go without them would bring trouble to all the island homes.

Now they came crowding in. The women who would not greet the boat earlier in the day had joined the other women of the island, together they formed a solid mass of mourning. They had seen the other boats come in from the mainland, and those wives who kept visitors in the summer months had been ready for the funeral since the first news of her death came in a message to Eddie at the post office. Billy Burke's wife, the woman who had come in as a girl from Murrisk, was one of them. From the wicket of the run where he had minded the hens since Mrs Dauntry left for the hospital Eddie heard her saying now, as she climbed the steps to the house door:

'She always reminded me of a woman I heard about once, over in Ennis. She was a lady poet, they said, and her hair was as yellow as ripe oats. She kept a small house there by the sea, and I was told if you could sit long enough in her kitchen the whole world would pass through it before your eyes. I never met her, mind. I'm only saying what I was told. But isn't that like Mrs Dauntry now? She brought the whole world to the island, in her time. I have to say it – I'm glad to have known her.'

Eddie heard how her voice was lost at last in the mill of people inside the house. He saw where the door was left open, it would be left open all night. People that he remembered, people he might have met, once, passed through it, and strangers came, he heard Dermot welcoming them, there was a sound of surprise, and he could hear Fr McGuinness talking as if he recognized people he had never met before. As the golden evening light wore down into dusk he heard Danny Joyce called on to sing – that was Fr McGuinness too, managing things, probably passing the whiskey with the rest. As the song rose Eddie recalled that it had been a favourite of Mrs Dauntry's, Danny Joyce knew that, and Eddie knew that he was standing to the song, rising it for her:

'I wish the Queen of England
Would write to me in time,
And put me in a uniform
All in my youth and prime.
I'd fight for Ireland's glory
From the clear daylight to the dawn
And I never would return again
For to plough the rocks of bawn.'

As tradition decreed, Danny Joyce dropped his voice and muttered the last couple of bars to end the song. Listening, Eddie did not hear a footstep until a scent caught him, a sweet light trace to undercut the hen-run smell. Drenched in a sweat of disbelief he turned, but it was only Ruth.

'I wondered where you were,' she said, holding out her hand.

He touched it and let it go. She hesitated, as if standing there with him against her will, but having nowhere else to go.

'It's getting very hot in there. There's such a crowd.'

He nodded, his eyes on the trellises of the high wall, the outside of the garden. He thought how he was going to live without her as part of his life. How was he going to live?

The young woman spoke suddenly, desperately:

'I loved her too, you know! I did love her!'

He looked at her at last. He was the only one who could make what had happened any different for her.

'Yes,' he said, the word heavy, she had to believe he believed what he was saying.

'Yes. She told me that. She always felt you loved her. Maybe, in your own way, as much as she loved you. She told me that.'

It may have been imagination. It may have been memory. It may have been true. The cloak of summer

204

night edged slowly along the coast of Mayo and on the island the lights were snapped on, doors closed, curtains drawn. Except at the high house where Mrs Dauntry lay and the door stood open to the air. From the mainland it would not be seen. No one there would see how the candles bloomed all night in her windows until they dissolved in the dawn. Their delicate anthers were radiant and steady, but they glowed against glass that shone to the west, on the dark side of the island, the unknown side.

THE END

The Killeen
Mary Leland

'Sheer good writing in the traditional narrative manner'
THE GUARDIAN

A killeen is a small graveyard, often situated at a crossroads. It was customary to bury the bodies of unbaptised babies there and the little cemeteries can still be found throughout the Irish countryside.

In Mary Leland's novel, set in Cork in the 1930s, the killeen can be seen as Ireland itself, in its early years as an independent state, an emergent nation still inhospitable to individual aspirations. And it is against the harsh background of the new republic that the overlapping story of three young people is played out.

'Mary Leland in this book has opened a dozen doors for the imagination; her shadowy people in their vivid landscape will haunt as ghostly figures always do. It is a story of people who love, but it is in no way a love story. Those who love most lose most, and that is possible the most haunting memory of all in this finely crafted book.'
MAEVE BINCHY, IRISH TIMES

'Her grasp of the vulnerability and inner strength of human beings is noteworthy.'
SUSAN HILL, GOOD HOUSEKEEPING

0 552 99203 8

BLACK SWAN

Ellen
Ita Daly

As an only child of Catholic Dublin parents, Ellen was a strange, solitary girl. She was lumpish and dull, she was lonely. But she had resigned herself to this, and wanted nothing more from life than to be left alone in her isolation, to carry out a quiet typing job without interference, without change. If only her mother would stop entertaining such ambitious fantasies for her. When Ellen's hopes of an academic career fell through, Mrs Yates moved on to visions of a glittering social success, inviting strange girls around for elaborate teas and friendships which never materialized.

The Ellen met Myra. Pretty, rosy Myra who wanted Ellen to be her friend, to meet her family, to share a flat! A new world unfolded, a world which Ellen found completely voluptuous; evenings by the fire, fish and chip suppers, secrets shared with a friend — even if that friend could sometimes be casually brutal. Throughout the summer months, there were lazy days spent in the garden with Adrien, Myra's stockbroker boyfriend and his cousin. Bobbie even paid attention to Ellen. She had never imagined that life could be like this, and she wanted it to go on forever. Who would have thought that the idyll could be violated — let alone in the shocking way it was?

0 552 99251 8

BLACK SWAN

A SELECTION OF TITLES WITH IRISH INTEREST AVAILABLE FROM BLACK SWAN

THE PRICES SHOWN BELOW WERE CORRECT AT THE TIME OF GOING TO PRESS. HOWEVER TRANSWORLD PUBLISHERS RESERVE THE RIGHT TO SHOW NEW RETAIL PRICES ON COVERS WHICH MAY DIFFER FROM THOSE PREVIOUSLY ADVERTISED IN THE TEXT OR ELSEWHERE.

☐ 99054 X	BORSTAL BOY	*Brendan Behan*	£3.95
☐ 99251 8	ELLEN	*Ita Daly*	£2.95
☐ 99203 8	THE KILLEEN	*Mary Leland*	£2.95
☐ 99256 9	SECTS AND OTHER STORIES	*John Morrow*	£3.95
☐ 99158 9	BRENDAN BEHAN	*Ulick O'Connor*	£2.95
☐ 99143 0	CELTIC DAWN	*Ulick O'Connor*	£4.95

All Black Swan Books are available at your bookshop or newsagent, or can be ordered from the following address:

Black Swan Books,
Cash Sales Department,
P.O. Box 11, Falmouth, Cornwall TR10 9EN

Please send a cheque or postal order (no currency) and allow 60p for postage and packing for the first book plus 25p for the second book and 15p for each additional book ordered up to a maximum charge of £1.90 in UK.

B.F.P.O. customers please allow 60p for the first book, 25p for the second book plus 15p per copy for the next 7 books, thereafter 9p per book.

Overseas customers, including Eire, please allow £1.25 for postage and packing for the first book, 75p for the second book, and 28p for each subsequent title ordered.